How NOT to Date a Demon

CAUTIONARY TAILS BOOK ONE

LANA KOLE

D1715083

For a complete list of content information pertaining to How Not to Date a Demon, please refer to my website.

For everyone who hates busy grocery stores.

Contents

1. Everything Is Fine

Maeve

"Take a breath. Everything is fine. Just... fine." With gritted teeth, Maeve repeated the mantra in her head as she stared at the latest sins her boyfriend had committed. The list was long and seemed to be growing every day.

"The sink is right here," she grumbled and snatched up the empty glass, rinsing it in her pristine sink before setting it on the previously empty drying rack.

How hard was that? Couldn't the man do one thing?

Maeve sighed as she dried her hands, glancing at the clock. It was nearing eleven, and he still hadn't made it home from the emergency he'd needed to stay late for, and wouldn't be for a while, if the text he'd just sent was any indication. Dinner had been scooped into little plastic containers hours ago.

They'd been dating for almost a year now, and yet she'd begun to feel as if they'd been married for thirty. All she did was clean up after him.

Sure, she knew he was stressed with work, but she had a job too, and she still managed to clean up after herself. Was it too much to ask for him to step it up a bit?

Maeve nodded. She could tell him that. Easy.

Can you do it nicely, though?

"Shush," she said aloud to the empty apartment.

She'd just tell him on a day when she wasn't ready to snap his head off. Applauding herself for such levelheadedness, she made her way to the bedroom. Galen knew she couldn't wait up for him. His hours were insane, and if his boss didn't give him a raise, she was going to personally march down there and kick his ass. She was tired of the waiting up and canceled dinners and postponed dates, and more than ready for Galen to have steady hours.

So she could actually have a boyfriend again.

With a sigh, she walked into the bathroom to begin her evening routine, stopping to put *someone's* socks in the basket where they'd been resting alongside it.

Just as she pulled the shower curtain to the side, a knock sounded on the door.

It preceded the jingle of keys, and she frowned. What was Galen doing home so early? His text had made it seem like she wouldn't see him for hours.

She entered the living room, aiming for the door, when it suddenly burst in. Three small shadows darted past her, and she gasped before turning to see what the hell Galen had done.

Three *puppies*—real life fucking puppies—danced and romped around the living room, stopping to smell every piece of furniture within reach.

Slowly, she lifted her gaze to her boyfriend. Galen, unaware of the thin edge of patience he was already scaling, held out a bouquet of flowers.

Even as her annoyance grew sharper, she couldn't help but appreciate the unfairly sexy sight of him, his black on black suit framing his shape perfectly.

"I am so sorry for being late for dinner. I convinced him to let me go early. Am I too late?"

Maeve slowly took the flowers from him and turned toward the kitchen. Stepping over too-excited puppies in the way, she made it to the sink to fill a vase with water for the carnations and roses. *Her favorites.*

Her chest tightened as she watched the vase fill, and organizing her thoughts was proving to be impossible.

Shaking her head, she turned to face Galen as he followed her in, stopping by the table.

"Puppies? What were you thinking?" she hissed quietly.

Galen frowned and took a step closer before he paused. His lips parted, but nothing came out. "Would you believe me if I said it was for work?"

Maeve shut the water off and leaned her hands on the edge of the sink, lowering her head. What the *actual* fuck?

"What kind of boss gives you three puppies to look after? Why?"

"They're... They're the puppies of his favorite dog, and he just wanted me to watch them for a week or two."

"A week or *two*?" she echoed. "Why?"

"He's going out of town, and they were going to be too much for his sitter, so he asked me. I didn't want to say no."

Maeve sighed, lowering her head into her hands and groaning in frustration.

"I hate your boss," she grumbled.

A soft touch brushed against her back, and when she didn't shrug it off, Galen rubbed his hand up her spine.

"What are we going to do with them? We don't have kennels, and they're gonna need so much care and attention. I just... can't dedicate the time to them that they need. We both work too much." Maeve's heart raced. They were still trying to sort their shit from moving in together, and now puppies?

But when she straightened her spine and turned to face him, he was staring at the cabinets, lip tucked between his teeth in thought. "I realize now I didn't think this through properly." He winced. "I understand. It was a spur of the moment thing. And besides, I know just where to take them."

A sigh of relief left her, but something was still... *off*. "You do? Will they be safe?"

Breaking the stare, he arched a brow at her. "If I said no, what would you do?"

Maeve rolled her eyes at him and narrowed her gaze. "I wouldn't just let you take them and dump them somewhere. They're so dumb and defenseless," she whined, waving a hand at them.

As if they knew she was talking about them, they turned their heads to her, their little yips trailing off into silence.

"Aw, don't say that, they're just babies!" Galen argued and dropped down to his knees.

The puppies just about tripped over themselves to get to him, pawing at him for attention.

"I know, I know," he cooed to them in a high-pitched voice. "It'll be okay, I promise. I'll take you guys to Jean's house, how about that?"

Maeve was going to melt into a puddle if he kept being *that* adorable with the puppies, and it took real effort to redirect her thoughts. "Who's Jean?" she asked, suspicion rising.

"He's a coworker who doesn't live too far from here."

A coworker? Warning bells went off in her head.

Maeve glared at him, his too-casual tone rubbing her wrong. "Is Jean the one who's been competing with you for this promotion?"

A long pause stretched between them before he finally nodded, rubbing one of the puppy's bellies.

How was she even going to tell the three of them apart?

"Is Jean watching the puppies going to give him more favor with the boss?"

Galen stood, and she lifted her head to stare up at him, not wanting to miss any minuscule hints in his expression.

He seemed reluctant to answer. "I don't want us to be stressed about them if we don't have to be. Don't agree to this just for me."

She sighed. "Will Jean get the promotion if he watches the puppies?"

"It's... possible. Though he explained to me that I hold the most favor because I helped him so much with the last project."

Maeve crossed her arms. She wanted him to get that promotion, she wanted stability and no more late nights and early mornings and long days.

Maeve wanted her boyfriend back. Devil be damned. And if the puppies were the key to that...

"Fine. They'll stay until your boss needs them back."

His eyes widened. "Really?"

Before Maeve could change her mind, she blurted, "Yes. I want this promotion for you. Fuck that guy. Jean."

"Are you sure?" he asked again, stepping closer and tilting her head up to him.

Maeve drew in a deep breath, Galen's hands warm against her cheeks. "Boss sucks, I know," he agreed. "But with him being gone the next two weeks, I can work from home and help out, keep an eye on them."

Maeve paused, grinding her teeth. Why hadn't he led with that information? If she knew he was actually going to be around to help…

You didn't exactly give him a chance to tell you.

Rolling her eyes at herself, she nipped at Galen's hand. "You should have led with that. Sorry I didn't give you the chance to. I'm just frustrated about stuff."

Galen lowered his hands, pulling her into his arms. She buried her head into his chest and inhaled his scent. It felt like the first deep breath she'd had all day.

"I love your temper. It's hot," he said with a chuckle.

She snorted. "You're such a dork."

"Remember our first date?" Galen asked and pulled back, a wistful smile curling his lips.

Color rushed to Maeve's cheeks at the memory. "How could I forget?"

What was supposed to be a movie and dinner date—original, right?—turned into a disaster before they'd even met one another.

"The first time I caught sight of you, you were on your tiptoes, yelling at the guy who hit your car and two seconds away from—"

"—kicking his ass. I know," Maeve answered with a sigh. They were really doing this memory lane thing.

Galen's embrace was warm, and she hid her pink cheeks in his chest, listening to his heartbeat. Her heart squeezed as she let herself get dragged down memory lane.

Galen had been such a sight the first time she'd seen him, practically glowing.

Of course, looking back now, she realized he'd simply been illuminated by the headlights of the cars behind her.

It went like this:

The driver who'd ultimately rear-ended her deserved it. Following her all the way down the road, he stayed right up on her bumper and urged her to go faster.

So Maeve had done the opposite.

But as she watched his lights splash over the same asphalt of the lot she was turning into, her nerves began rattling. She was so paranoid that when a car backed out of its space, she was too distracted to notice and almost collided with it. Thankfully, she tapped her brakes at the last second.

And just as she'd rolled to a stop from a whopping six miles an hour, she was bumped from behind. The very specific metallic and plastic *thunk* of their cars colliding was like music to her ears.

"Haha, that's what you get, asshole," she jeered from the safety of her car. Throwing it in park, she grabbed her info, pushed open her door, and got out to meet this jerk. Pausing by the bumper of her car, she waited.

It was a long moment before the door to his giant truck opened, and he dropped to the ground with a smug grin.

She already had her insurance card out. "If you didn't ride my ass so hard, I bet you wouldn't have hit me."

The smug grin melted away into open-mouthed shock, as if he couldn't believe she'd spoken to him that way. At five foot three, she got that a lot, but being tiny came with plenty of rage. However... she was supposed to be meeting her date here, so she would try her best to keep a lid on it.

Calm. Serene. Rational.

With a tight smile, she held out her insurance card. "I don't have a lot of time, so here's my info. I just need yours."

The man matched his truck, in boots and a worn ball cap, complete with the pouch of dip extending his bottom lip.

He crossed his arms. "What's the rush? You didn't seem to be in a hurry on the way here."

Maeve collected herself with a deep breath. It was already past seven, the time the movie was supposed to start. Was her date inside waiting already? What if he thought she stood him up?

"Now you're just holding us both up. Want to get this over with or not?" she bit out.

"Well now, I'm not so sure." He paused, and his slimy gaze slid down her form. Her lip curled in distaste. "Knowing a little hottie like you was behind the wheel, I'd be willing to ride your ass some more."

Maeve let his words soak in for a moment, feeling her cheeks heat.

"Aw, got you blushing?" he teased.

Maeve flicked her insurance card at him, and watched it flutter to the asphalt by his boots. "What a generous offer, assuming you can fuck better than you drive." She let her brows dip as if a thought occurred to her. "Of course, with that micro you're carrying, I doubt anyone gets a happy ending." She tapped her wrist with two fingers. "Now can we please get on with this? Or do we need to file an official report as well, hm?"

She dipped her head down to glance at the damage on her car. The ding wasn't even that bad, and she did *not* want to waste her evening waiting on the police. But she'd be willing, if only to inconvenience this asshole.

When she faced the yeehaw guy again, his face was red, and he was slowly lowering his arms.

"Aw, got you blushing?" She threw his own words back at him, her tone sharp as a knife.

"Why, you little bitch," he shouted, taking a threatening step forward.

Maeve tensed, barely holding back the urge to spring toward him.

Their gazes met, and she watched the situation process behind his eyes. Was he really about to attack her over a little dick comment?

She snickered at her own thoughts without meaning to. But it slipped out and oh—

That must have pissed him off, because he committed, rushing toward her. Maeve froze, waited until he was close enough, but not quite at arm's reach, and twisted just out of the way. He must not have expected it, and adrenaline buzzed through her veins as he slammed a hand into her car to stop himself. She leapt at the chance, literally, and jumped on his back, latching her left arm around his throat and locking it in by crooking her forearm across the opposite wrist.

He garbled a curse at her and flailed around, and Maeve went for a spin around the parking lot with a squeak of alarm.

This yeehaw guy was pretty big. If he slammed her into the back of his truck or something, it could knock her out.

Maybe she should have thought of that first.

Oops.

"Can you just chill out?" she shouted in his ear. "What the hell's wrong with you?"

She reaffirmed her grip and squeezed her knees on either side of his waist. As he spun again, she realized his truck was nearing, and she braced herself for impact, but—

A pair of arms wrapped around her waist, interrupting the yeehaw's spin, and pulled her away like she weighed nothing, just before yeehaw could slam her into his vehicle.

Maeve glanced over her shoulder to find an impossibly tall, dark-haired man above her who looked eerily like the guy in the profile picture she was supposed to meet.

"Well, never thought I'd meet you like this. Hi, Maeve, I'm Galen."

Oh.

He *was* the guy from the app she was supposed to meet.

Maeve's cheeks heated—from embarrassment this time—and she chuckled lamely as Galen lowered her to the ground.

Once she was flat-footed again, she turned to face the scene of the crime.

Yeehaw's face was red, his hat was gone, and he looked pissed. But one glance at the towering figure behind her, and he averted his gaze.

Without even exchanging another word, he leaned down to snatch her insurance card off the ground, got inside his truck, and pulled out a small white card.

"You guys are a match made in hell. Fuck off," he said, flicking his own card out the window. His truck came to life with a roar, and he backed out of the aisle, burning rubber on his way out of the lot.

When she turned to face her date, she found Galen grinning.

Maeve flushed under that smile. "This is embarrassing." Wiping the sweat off her brow, she avoided his gaze as she asked, "Still interested in that date?"

Galen didn't answer at first, and she finally lifted her eyes to his. They were dark and intense and totally didn't match the smile on his face. "With you? *Very* interested."

Maeve cocked her head to the side. After that regal display in the theater parking lot? This guy had to be crazier than even her.

Honk!

The horn of a car blared, startling both of them out of their stares.

"Get parked, I'll go inside and get the drinks and popcorn. Requests?"

He bent and picked the card up for her like a perfect gentleman. Maeve told him her drink request, and he grinned before heading toward the theater, walking backward.

"You're not gonna drive off without me, right?" he called out.

Heat rushed to her cheeks, keys jingling in her hands, and she was hyperaware of the car's lights blinding her as his horn beeped again.

"I'll see you inside!" she yelled back.

Galen finally turned around just in time to avoid face-planting into the glass doors and pushed his way inside.

Maeve had met him inside, and, well... the rest was history.

She really was a lucky girl.

And Galen was a lucky guy.

He better not forget it.

2. Memory Lane

Maeve

"Of course I do," she answered Galen with a huff, flashing the memory away. "It's hard to forget such an embarrassing first impression."

His dark eyes twinkled with mirth. "Embarrassing? Honey, that's how I *knew* you were the one for me."

Her heart flipped over in her chest, but she refused to be wooed by his pretty words. That didn't stop her from fighting the urge to curl her hair around her finger and draw her toe against the floor. "What do you mean by that?"

Galen rolled his eyes. "You know exactly what I mean. I couldn't have dreamed of a woman more perfect for me than you," he said, expression turning serious. "And I don't want to mess this up. What are you frustrated with? What can I do to help?"

Maeve frowned at him. She was supposed to be mad. Why'd he have to come in and be so... so rational?

"First, you can get these guys settled in for the night before they eat our apartment."

"Oh, come on, they aren't that bad," he urged, turning his back on her to watch the puppies as they ran around.

"Really?" she asked, tone heavy with sarcasm as she watched one of the puppies chew on her floor-length curtains while another chewed on that puppy's leg.

"Yeah, it'll be... fine," he said, sounding a little less confident. "Guys," he chided. "We talked about this."

The puppies ignored him, continuing their chaos with playful yelps of excitement.

Her lips tightened as she refused to show even an inch of give. They were not cute. They were evil little machines of destruction. Their floppy ears were *nothing* compared to the chaos.

His lips lost the curl of his smile, and it stung her heart. "We're living together now. I know it's different, and something neither of us are used to." He crooked two fingers at her. "So come on, I'm a big boy. How can I make the transition easier?"

Maeve grabbed his two fingers and held them in her hand. "I don't wanna be too harsh."

But she had to be realistic. Maeve was tired of cleaning up after him.

He nodded, expression serious, as if he were taking mental notes. "You won't be. Just tell me. Don't make me beg."

But you're so hot when you beg.

Maeve. Now is now the time, you horny goblin.

With a chuckle, she met his gaze. "Put your stuff where it belongs. Dirty clothes in the hamper, not beside it. Dishes in the sink. Snacks back in the cabinet. I like my counters without clutter."

Galen winced. "I'm really bad at that, I'm sorry. I took care of my shit at home, but I guess it's not fair of me to expect you to just because you're... here. I'll make more of an effort from now on, I promise."

Cute little snarls and innocent growls sounded from the living room. When had they even run off?

Heart warming at the sounds, Maeve found the source of the playful grunts and whines as she leaned over the back of the couch to find the puppies all tussling between the coffee table and the couch.

All three of them were black, with the most adorable pink dotted noses. Again, how did she tell them apart?

"They are cute, aren't they?" Galen teased.

Maeve sighed as one flopped over onto... *his* back, pink little belly displayed as his brothers hopped on top of him and chewed on his ears and feet with playful nips.

"Unfortunately, they are. But if you don't get the promotion after this..." She sucked in a deep breath. "I will personally pay him a visit."

He began to chuckle, his lips curling into another one of her favorite smiles. "That's why you're perfect for me. Willing to take your rage out on anyone who needs it."

Galen reached out a hand and pulled her toward him, wrapping her in his arms. He smelled warm and spicy, delicious.

"Someone's got to," she mumbled into his shirt.

He started chuckling, chest shaking against her, and she pulled back, ready to be insulted and lean into him. "Sorry, sorry, bad timing," he apologized. "But I was just remembering, when I grabbed you off that guy... you just, you deactivated like a cat or something."

He laughed again, the sound deep and rumbly, and yet it sent chills dancing across her skin, and how dare he possess such dichotomy?

What else was Maeve supposed to do but laugh with him, reliving the moment all over again.

Their giggles subsided and she stared up at him, remembering how he'd been a perfect gentleman the entire evening until she'd invited him in. Then, of course, he'd fucked her ten ways to Sunday and, well, she couldn't let him go after that.

"You know, if you didn't have three puppies to figure out how to keep from causing mayhem, maybe I'd let you apologize a little more... physically."

His expression was absolutely crestfallen when she pulled away.

With an evil little grin, she pecked him on the lips and wished them all a good night before she retreated to her puppy free room and crawled between the sheets.

Wakefulness came to her slowly. It crept along her senses and tickled her just enough for Maeve to blink her eyes open.

Galen was warm beside her, his breaths steady and even.

She yawned. Why the hell was she awake at...

Glancing at the clock, she blinked her blurry vision into focus, finding an ungodly three-fifteen awaiting her.

With a quiet sigh, she let her head relax back on the pillow and glanced around the dark room.

A shuffle of nails across the hardwood floor startled her, and she sat up—

And promptly froze.

By the door to the bedroom were three matching pairs of... *red*, glowing eyes staring in her direction.

Well... at least they weren't chewing on her curtains.

Eyes wide, sure she was still dreaming, she lay back down and stared at the ceiling.

What the fuck?

She shuffled closer to Galen in the bed, seeking his warmth for comfort. He mumbled something and rolled over, making room for her to snuggle up.

He curled an arm around her back, and she sighed in relief. She felt safe like this, and she blinked sleepily, her thoughts dispersing as the veil of sleep grew heavier. She couldn't even remember why she'd woken up in the first place.

And why was she worried about being safe?

A click of nails across the hardwood floor startled her awake again, and she remembered.

The puppies were guarding the door.

It would have been cute if their fucking eyes weren't so bright red they were casting shadows along the floor.

"S'not natural," she mumbled incoherently as sleep pulled her back under.

Galen's arms tightened around her, and she couldn't fight it anymore.

Waking up the next morning was much easier with the sun streaming in through their curtains. An uneasy knot was still bunched in her chest, and she sat up to an empty bed and an empty room.

The door was closed, and there was no sign of the three puppies.

Maybe that was just a dream last night. Her anxiety over the three puppies manifesting while she was asleep.

Yeah, that was it.

"Makes more sense than glowing eyes, doesn't it?" she muttered to herself.

She stretched and pulled herself from the bed, yawning as she opened the door and found an empty apartment.

Frowning, she retreated to her bedside table and checked her phone, but there was no message from Galen. Wasn't he working from home now? Where was he?

With a sigh, she dropped her phone to the bed and made her way to the bathroom. She stripped and held her sleep clothes over the hamper. A flash of one of Galen's shirts caught her eye, and she smiled as she pulled it out. He was already doing better.

She was about to drop it back in when she noticed a tear in the fabric.

"Oh no," she said, holding out the last syllable in disappointment as she dropped her clothes and held up his shirt. He really liked this shirt.

From the front, it didn't seem any different, but when she turned it around, she frowned.

"What the hell?" she asked aloud.

Two matching rips ran in the fabric parallel to each other, right between the shoulder blades. How the hell had he managed that?

Shaking her head and reminding herself to ask him for the story later, she finished readying for the day and took it with her to toss in the trash.

It wasn't until she entered the kitchen that she found a sticky note scrawled with Galen's sloppy script.

"Gone for a bit, took the pups so they didn't wake you up. Be back soon," she read aloud.

Well, that was sweet.

And even the dishes from their failed dinner were already taken from the dishwasher and put away.

On top of that, when she opened the fridge, a large mug of coffee with her name on it—literally, he'd written it on a heart shaped sticky note—sat in the middle like an offering.

Galen was already doing better. And talking to him had been so easy. He hadn't offered excuses or tried to argue with her. He'd listened and thought about what she said and promised to improve.

And so far, he was doing a good fucking job.

Now the question was, would it last?

3. Offensive Wardrobe

Galen

G alen shushed the puppies once more, giving their leads a gentle tug as he pulled the keys out for the apartment.

But before he could even push one into the lock, the door swung open to Maeve's smile.

"You're back!"

The excitement on her face was bright and genuine, making her green eyes sparkle, and he was struck stupid for a second.

The three puppies weren't, and they tried to rush into the apartment. The new lead he had tied to their matching harnesses pulled them to a stop.

One of them plopped over dramatically, and even Maeve was helpless in the presence of their cuteness. She giggled, the sound light and airy and welcoming, and he followed her in like another lost puppy, plastic bags rustling in his hands.

"Spoiling them already?" she asked with an arched brow.

He paused, glancing up guiltily, at least until he saw the mirth in her pretty green eyes. "I had to drop by the office, and took them with me."

"Well," she prompted, "show me what you got."

Galen smiled and let her take one of the bags and set them on the couch.

He unsnapped the puppies from the leash and watched as they waddled around uncoordinated in their harnesses.

"So... do they have names?" she asked as she took a seat.

"Of course. The one over there" —he pointed to the one in the green harness who was sticking his nose into the bag— "that's Bubba, short for Beezlebub. The girl in blue is Achlys. Or Lissie. And the last one in purple is Eligos, or Eli."

Maeve blinked at him, a smile twitching on her lips. "Those are certainly... name choices. Do they have a preference?"

He rolled his eyes, a pinch of affection fluttering in his chest. "I know they're weird names, so I shortened them myself. They seem to take to them better, watch."

He snapped his fingers and called, "Lissie, come here, Lissie!"

The pup's head snapped in his direction, pulling her attention from the coffee table. Her ears flopped side to side as she waddled over like a big fluffball.

His heart melted, and he sat on the couch to reach down and scoop her up. She wiggled in his arms, but as soon as he settled her on his lap, she started nipping at his hands and seeking affection.

"That's the cutest thing I've ever seen," Maeve said quietly.

Galen grinned and leaned down to kiss Lissie's little furry head. "See?" he whispered loudly. "I told you she'd give in."

"Galen," she chided with a laugh. "Shush."

"Okay, okay," he conceded, his attention all for the puppies as the other two trampled over to see what their sister was up to.

Galen grinned, watching them play before he could help himself. These were the cutest damned pups he'd ever seen. How could Maeve have considered not keeping them?

"You're just so cute. Yes you are," he cooed.

If only his colleagues could see him now.

"You're soft," Maeve said with a chuckle as she rearranged the bags. The words were a little too close to something his coworkers would say for comfort.

"So what?" he asked, glancing up at her. She was a vision. Dark hair long and glossy over her shoulders, lips pink and quirked with a smile.

Galen slid to the floor with all three puppies, his back resting against the front of the couch as he waved his hands back and forth between the pups. They chased his hand, mouths open wide, little teeth bared, ears flopping all over the place.

"I'm allowed to be soft. What psychopath isn't soft for puppies? Huh?" he asked one of the pups in question, leaning down for wet kisses.

"I never knew you loved dogs so much," Maeve said, sitting down beside him.

She giggled as Bubba trotted over and flopped down over her crossed legs, still kicking to get to her.

"Well, these are a little different."

If only she knew how different.

"Yeah, yeah, they're still small and cute, I know. Alright, show me the haul," she requested again.

Her attention was still on the midnight fluffball in her lap, but he pulled one of the bags closer anyway.

Chew toys, food bowls, a big bed for them to share—

"Yeah! Maybe we can set it by the bed." She waved her hand toward the bedroom. "Last night, they were sleeping by the door."

Already?

"Perfect spot for it then," he agreed, eager to change the subject. "I figure since I'm going to be home, we won't need kennels. I'll just keep an eye on them. And they did okay last night without a kennel."

Maeve chewed her lip as she glanced from Galen to the pups and back again.

"Alright, fine. But if they chew up our curtains, I want new ones."

"Of course," he agreed readily. "Speaking of chewing... I'm pretty sure it's breakfast time for them."

He picked Lissie up as he stood, and she wiggled in his arms until he put her down in the kitchen.

Maeve's gaze was heavy on him, and he wondered briefly if she'd forgiven him yet and was ready for that physical apology she'd mentioned las—

"By the way, I noticed you did some stuff around the apartment this morning. I appreciate it. But what happened to that shirt in the hamper?"

Galen's back was to her as he pulled bowls and their food out of the plastic bags, and he tried to hide his alarm. He'd meant to throw it away.

"What do you mean?" he asked.

"It just had two huge gashes in it. On the back," she continued. Her tone sounded innocent. Maybe she was oblivious.

That was all he could ask for.

"Maybe one of the pups did it while I was carrying them? I don't remember getting caught on anything," he lied. He knew exactly where those gashes had come from, but the last person he could tell was Maeve.

At least... not yet.

Not until things were ready.

"Oh, okay. Weird. I threw it out, I hope that's okay?"

"Of course," he said over his shoulder as he sat the three bowls out. "Sorry, I guess I just didn't notice. That's so weird." Was he talking about it too much? Should he apologize again? Fuck.

His stomach churned. He hated lying to her. *Hated it.* But he had no choice—he couldn't tell her yet. Not only would it endanger her, but... he might lose her.

Galen wasn't ready for that. Probably wouldn't ever be.

"Don't worry about it," she said absentmindedly. "I know you have plenty of extras," she teased.

He paused from his task of feeding the pups, grateful for the distraction. "Are you saying my wardrobe is all the same?"

"What? That would be crazy," she answered dryly. "It's not like the only color you ever wear is black."

Galen glanced down at his clothes. This was one of his finer suits, but yes, still black. He lifted one side of his jacket out. "There's color," he argued, motioning to the gold lining of the jacket.

Her gaze dripped over him from head to toe, and he loved when her eyes went dark like that. Maeve was weak for him in a suit, and he was just as weak for her, for pleasing her.

"Besides," he continued, "It's not like you can say much else." Galen was far too excited about being right as she glanced down at her own clothes and found an oversized black shirt.

"The shirt belongs to you, so it doesn't count," she retorted.

Galen sat the bowls down and grinned as the puppies rushed to claim their food.

While they were busy, he washed his hands and glanced over his shoulder.

"It looks better on you anyway."

She arched a brow at him and leaned against the doorway. "Is that so?"

Galen turned, making his way around the kitchen island and stalking his way toward the entrance. Toward the woman taunting him while looking far too delicious in his clothes.

Her fingers tightened around the hem, and she fluttered it over her thighs to tease him.

"Maeve," he warned, pulse speeding up as she smiled at him.

"Hmm?" With her plump smile bitten between her teeth, she began walking backwards. He followed her slowly, as if she was a siren and he a lonely sailor.

At the look in her eyes, he darted toward her, and she took off with a squeal. Heart pounding, he raced after her like a madman. However, karma had different plans as the three puppies joined in on playtime and nipped at his ankles. Staggering, he hopped from foot to foot to avoid stepping on the clumsy pups, right up until he tripped.

He crashed to the floor, and the puppies pounced, tails wagging and excited yelps blending with Maeve's giggles to echo around their home.

Their home.

He'd never felt more comfortable anywhere else with any other person. He sighed, the smitten man that he was, and cleared his throat.

"Darling, you have exactly ten seconds to get to the bedroom before I carry you there."

Sitting up, he met her gaze and saw a flash of heat before she took off.

He made a production with the way he got up, thumping his heeled boots down with each step for dramatic effect. The puppies spilled off him and leapt around until he snapped his fingers at them.

They stilled, sitting on their haunches and staring up at him.

"Be good," he said simply.

The puppies trotted off past him, and seconds later, he heard the kibbles from their bowls skittering around as they ate.

Finally, with no distractions in his way, he crossed the hardwood floor to the bedroom with the door cracked. He paused with his hand on the doorframe and pressed a finger against the wooden door.

It swung open slowly, revealing Maeve in the middle of their bed, legs splayed wide as the hand between her thighs moved rhythmically.

"What's this?" he asked, voice low.

The heat Maeve always stirred within him sparked from embers into the initial flickers of a flame.

She lifted her head up, eyes half-lidded as she let her hand fall away, granting him a teasing glance before she folded her thighs together.

"It's been more than ten seconds," she explained. "I got bored."

He hummed and closed the door behind himself, stalking forward and placing two palms on the edge of the bed before he crawled toward Maeve.

She was wearing one of his black shirts and nothing else. With a low growl, he caged her in with his arms and legs and stared down at her. Heat flared in her gaze, and she bit her lip in the most infuriatingly hot way.

Unable to resist, he leaned down and soothed the abused flesh, lips soft and warm against his.

Kissing Maeve always felt a little like he was selling his soul.

He knew he shouldn't, but goddamn, the possibilities of what was to come were too good for him to resist.

Hopefully, her first.

"Got yourself all worked up, hmm? Need some help?"

Gaze darkening in challenge, Maeve smirked and spread her thighs beneath him. "You know I love this suit," she purred.

Shit, the things this woman did to him.

He tasted her just like he wanted. Every inch of her, from her lips to her hip bones to the insides of her thighs. And finally, when he'd teased her enough, he swiped his tongue between her folds, tasting the effect he had on her.

"That's my girl," he whispered. "So wet for me."

Her lips parted on a silent moan as she tried to cant her hips in his direction.

Stilling her with an arm atop each thigh, he lowered his head again and feasted.

He licked and lapped between her folds, teasing and pulling back at the last second. And he didn't stop until her fingers were tangled in his hair, nails digging into his scalp, moans falling from her lips in the most delicious sounding whines.

"Galen," she said, but his name trailed off into a moan as he tweaked a nipple and swiped his tongue inside her one last time.

"Yes, my dear?" he asked with a smug grin.

Maeve tilted her head up. "You've still got some groveling to do. But for now... I want you inside me."

That was a sacrifice Galen was willing to make.

4. Strike One

Maeve

Maeve wasn't comfortable. With a sigh, she rolled over again and attempted to find the perfect spot amongst all her pillows, the blanket, and her boyfr—

She slid her hand over his side of the bed, meeting only cold sheets and cooler air.

Where the hell was he?

Blinking her eyes open, she adjusted to the soft moonlight and grabbed her phone off the nightstand.

It was three-thirty. So she had like four hours of sleep left.

Why had this become some kind of ritual for her lately? She used to sleep the whole night through.

She muffled a groan in the blanket and stopped at the sound of something in the other room.

Alarm ran through her, and she sat up, holding the covers to her chest. Listening harder, she recognized the sound of Galen's voice, and her panic eased.

A mischievous smile curled her lips as she slid her legs over the side of the bed. She couldn't wait to bust Galen and make endless fun of him for singing in the middle of the night. And to who? The puppies?

But the more she listened, the more she couldn't recognize what the hell he was singing. As she drew closer to the living room, the sound of his voice grew louder, but she didn't recognize the tune or the words of the song.

The moment suddenly felt so surreal, and she wrapped her hand around the doorknob. The hair on the back of her neck stood up, but her curiosity was stronger than whatever fight-or-flight instinct was trying to activate. The door opened silently, and she pulled it toward her to see through a small gap.

Galen was sitting on the living room floor, his back to her as he faced the three puppies. At first, her heart warmed, thinking he was singing them to sleep or something equally cheesy.

But she wouldn't quite classify it as singing. It wasn't... lyrical. His voice was low, and the longer she listened, the less sense it made. The shapes of the words weren't anything like English, or any other language she'd heard. But the puppies didn't seem to care, staring up at him in a daze, tongues lolling out as they panted normally.

But there wasn't anything normal about this. Not the sound, the dogs, or their red fucking eyes.

A shiver went up her spine as she listened a moment longer, the cadence of his voice akin to a chant.

Backing away, Maeve tried to stay silent as she shut the door behind her and tiptoed back to the bed.

It seemed colder than ever as she crawled beneath the cover and pulled it up to her chin.

Whatthefuckwhatthefuckwhatthefuck—

As her own chant echoed in her mind, she slammed her eyes shut and willed it all to go away.

That didn't happen, of course, but in the moment, she just needed to believe this was all just a dream and that she would wake up and everything would be normal, and she wouldn't have all these thoughts about her boyfriend and—

Maeve was asleep before she could even finish the thought.

But not for long, as consciousness swam at the edges of sleep once again by a shuffling in the bed.

She rolled over, coming face-to-face with Galen, who was wiping sleep away.

"I'm twisted like a pretzel over here," he groaned, and it was only then Maeve felt the warmth against her calf.

Glancing down the length of the bed, she spied three blobs of shadow snoring away peacefully.

"Galen!" she hissed, barely awake. They weren't supposed to be on the bed, and he knew it!

"What?" The word came out a half whine, half sleepy grumble. "You said keep them from being destructive. Can't destruct if they're asleep."

One's ear was flopped over his head, and she sighed. "Fine, but only because they're keeping me warm."

She didn't even recall the weird chanting until the next morning, when she'd snuck out of bed to get ready for work. The hottest coffee warmed her throat and soul as she drank it down, preparing to answer phone calls all day in tech support.

Thrilling.

But with caffeine came clarity, and her smile faded as she remembered Galen sitting in the living room, heard the eerie chants, saw the shadows cast by glowing eyes all over again.

Her eye twitched.

Like, what the fuck?

Maeve didn't even know what to think of it. What sense did it make?

Routine was her coping mechanism, so like always, she sat her mug down to empty the coffee grounds from her brew into the trash. Was Galen just some weirdo, and she'd only recently been able to see it? Surely her glasses weren't that rose colored, were they?

With a huff, she stepped on the pedal to snap the trash can lid open—and froze.

Galen had taken the trash out last night. So *why* was there a black shirt in the bin?

Her bullshit meter went off as she pinched the shirt with two fingers and slowly lifted it from the trash. She dumped the coffee grounds and spread the shirt out, looking for the same—

Yep.

Two gashes parallel to each other, inches apart, were ripped into the fabric.

"Why is there another one?" she murmured.

It *was* another one, right?

Maeve peeled the neck down and eyed the brand, trying to remember if the other shirt was the exact same. But why would he have dug it out of the trash when Maeve had tossed it, only to put it back in? The only way it made sense is if it was a different shirt. With the same tears.

What would tear a shirt in that spot?

She couldn't help the vision that flashed through her mind, a movie they'd seen together months ago, painfully cheesy with its horror effects, the werewolf ripping right through his clothes as he changed from human to wolf.

You're being ridiculous.

Shaking her head, she dropped it back in and dusted her hands off. Then she pulled the bag out and tied it up. After washing her hands thoroughly, she grabbed her travel mug, sling bag, and trash before giving the bedroom door another glance.

Between the shirts and the weird chanting and the three dogs... what the hell, Galen?

After dumping the bag in the building's dumpster, she promised to have a good day at work. No distractions.

It didn't take long for her to break that promise though.

"Miss Betty, are you asking me to tell you how to use the device?" she questioned, lowering her head into her hands.

The old lady sputtered on the other end. "W-Well, no. That would be strange, wouldn't it, dear? I just... haven't ever used one of these toys before," she explained, sounding absolutely scandalized.

How did Maeve's life come to this? Explaining how to use a vibrating dildo to an old lady somewhere in the world. She was tech support, not sex education.

It was so ridiculous, she let out a silent giggle. If someone was going to have a good day, it clearly wasn't Maeve. So why not Miss Betty?

"Miss Betty, did you know there are over eight thousand nerve endings in the clitoris alone? That's double the number of those in a penis."

"Oh my," she said.

"And the toy you have in your hands is made to stimulate every one of them."

"Oh *my*," she repeated.

"Now, do you see the bunny ears above the power button?"

Miss Betty gasped. "Those are bunny ears? How precious."

Maeve couldn't help but laugh.

In between calls, she listed off all the weird shit she'd begun to notice about her boyfriend.

The torn shirts, the chanting, the three puppies with glowing eyes. Their freaky names?

Maeve deflated as she looked at her list. It was too vague.

She needed more. More... weirdness.

Because at this point... she didn't know where to start. Who was Galen?

Or what? her subconscious supplied.

"Stop it," she whispered to herself. There was no need to get carried away here. No such thing as werewolves.

But what if it wasn't a werewolf? What if it was some other creature?

Shut up!

She closed the tabs on her computer, scribbled out her sticky note list before crumpling it. Tossing it in the shred bin, she collected herself and put the thoughts from her mind.

She could deal with it later.

Unfortunately, *later* came sooner than she anticipated, and always at the worst time. The sound of the bedroom door creaking open and closed pulled her from sleep. Again.

Could she not get an entire fucking night's worth?

She blinked her eyes open, sitting up as unease slithered through her.

Galen froze on his way to the bed, shirtless and in his sweats. He was... glistening?

"Hot cakes, why are you sweating?" she asked, voice tumbling out like pea gravel. She cleared her throat from sleep.

"What?"

Maeve watched as he wiped a hand across his forehead before seeing the moisture and nodding. "Oh, uh, I woke up from a bad dream. Yeah, that's why I went to the kitchen to get some water. Want some?" He held a glass out to her, and she noticed the slightest shake in his hand, water sloshing against the rim.

What kind of dream had it been?

Shaking her head, she patted the spot beside her in the bed, concern brushing away cobwebs of sleep.

"What was the dream about?"

He winced, darting his gaze from hers, brows furrowing. Maeve had never seen him like this. What had him so shaken up?

"It was... uh, about my job, I think," he said, clearing his throat.

She went into comfort mode, her worries and suspicions forgotten in the face of Galen's clear distress. Maeve had known he'd been worried about the promotion, but worried enough for him to have nightmares?

"You poor thing," she cooed, and took the glass from him.

He blinked at her emptily, and her heart melted. "Come back to bed."

Galen let her pull his bulk into the bed, and she sat on his lap, curled around him, wrapping her arms around his shoulders and holding him close.

Her boobs did make the best pillows. Galen's words, not hers.

"It'll work out just fine. And if not, then we'll figure it out together."

Galen lifted his head, peered at her, and they were both quiet for a long time.

"You mean that, don't you?" Galen asked.

It made her lips curl into a frown. Did he not believe her? "Of course."

His gaze softened as he stared at her, the lines around his eyes fading away. "Just knowing that helps," he said in a rough voice.

Then he pulled her close again, and she rested her chin atop his head and stroked her fingers through his hair. "Everything will work out how it's supposed to," she whispered.

"I hate when you say that," he retorted, his voice little more than a vibration against her chest.

It pulled a chuckle from her, and Galen scooped his hand around her waist and rolled them over.

"Sleep," he mumbled and pulled the blankets up around them. She cozied up to him, seeking his warmth.

"Goodnight, baby," he whispered.

Maeve drew circles on his chest until she felt his breath even out, and only then did she let sleep suck her back under.

5. The List

Maeve

Maeve got up early.

Shocking, right?

She crawled out of bed silently and slinked around the house to make breakfast for Galen. But coffee first, of course. Rain tapped against the windows, making it the perfect day to sleep in since she had the day off. But she could sleep *after* she spoiled her boyfriend. Galen was stressed, and Maeve had been too caught up in her own shit to notice.

So she added powdered sugar to the French toast for an extra treat.

And since it was raining, she even stopped by the front door to check that there was an umbrella and a jacket for Galen to wear if he had to drop by the office.

The umbrella was folded and hanging on the bottom row. "Ah," she said absently, and shuffled closer to grab it—

Her foot landed in something wet. And cold.

At first, she could *only* assume it was from a puppy, and she groaned. But when she flicked the light on and glared a little closer, she realized it was just water.

"Galen," she whined quietly. "Why'd you hang your jacket up *here* when it was wet..." Maeve trailed off.

Galen wasn't up yet. He was still sleeping peacefully in bed, like he had all night...

Maeve remembered Galen being slick with sweat in the middle of the night.

But what if it wasn't sweat?

Her gaze went to the window, to the sidewalk darkened with rain and leaves and sticks from the storm that had moved in sometime during the night.

What if it had been rain?

Where would he have gone?

Maeve fondled all the jackets, but they were dry. However, when had she woken up? It had been at least two hours ago. That was enough time for the jacket to drip dry, leaving behind the puddle. Right?

You're overthinking. Relax.

Maeve took a deep breath. Calm. Collected. Reasonable.

"Honey bun?" Galen's soft voice was suddenly right by her ear, and she squeaked, jumping to the side.

"Oh my god!" she exclaimed, heart thumping against her chest. "Shorten my life, why don't you?"

Galen winced, though his lips were curled in a smile. "Sorry. You were staring into space. You okay?"

"What?" How long had she been standing there? "Yes, yes, I'm fine. Just thinking. Good morning," she greeted, trying to sound more like a normal girlfriend and not one who suspected Galen was somehow a supernatural creature or cheating on her just because of a puddle.

"I made breakfast," she announced.

His eyes widened. "Is that what smells so good? What'd you make?"

Pointing toward the kitchen, she stepped around Galen. "Come and see! Coffee?"

Before he could answer, Maeve grabbed his pre-doctored mug of bliss and turned back to face him.

"Wow. Did I win boyfriend of the year award or something? What's all this for?"

Well, this was all planned before I realized you were possibly lying.

Kill him with kindness.

Did we decide he's guilty?

No. Yes. No. Maybe?

Maeve shook her teetering thoughts away and told him the reason she'd woken up early. "Well, I felt kinda bad after you had your nightmare. I didn't know you were *that* stressed, and I can't believe it took a nightmare for me to notice. So... this is kind of my apology. And I just wanted you to start the day off right."

"Maeve," he said, dragging out her name. He sat his coffee down and braced his hands on either side of the island, pinning her in. "The only thing that would make this day even more perfect is if you kissed me."

Maeve was weak, staring up at his still wrinkled bed face and messy hair. Who was she to deny him?

Leaning up on her toes, she pressed her lips to Galen's for a brief kiss.

He pouted, so she went back for another, sweeter one.

"Did you sleep better after your nightmare?" she asked as she pulled away. Maeve spun out of his arms and grabbed his plate to set on the bar.

"Huh—Oh. Yeah, like a baby," he answered.

The small hesitation made her stomach twist, but she let it go.

For now.

"No, I can't. I shouldn't. Right?"

Maeve threw her hands up in the air and went for another lap around the kitchen island. Her laptop was sitting on the island counter, open to a search engine. The cursor was blinking at her, daring her to type in what she wanted to know, but she felt...

"This is so stupid," she grumbled and whirled around. The train of puppies on her trail tripped over one another as they tried and failed to come to a clumsy stop.

"What do I do?" she asked them. Three innocent, clueless pairs of eyes stared up at her. Not glowing, she might add.

Maybe she'd imagined the eyes. Maybe she'd imagined it all.

No. Those shirts had been ripped in very specific, suspicious places that made her think of old werewolf movies from the 80s.

Why? How?

One of the pups barked at her, a tiny ruff that was so adorable it melted her heart. Maeve turned to stare at the computer, the blinking cursor.

Cuddling Galen back to sleep, feeling his arms around her, knowing that he needed her, was enough for her to want to give this whole thing up.

And it was that thought exactly that made her pull out her laptop as soon as Galen left the apartment. She couldn't get swept up in... in her tall, dark, super sexy boyfriend that she was totally head over heels for.

She couldn't keep brushing off all these weird things that kept happening. And with the 'nightmare' and the jacket that was *maybe* wet.

The puppies weren't paying her any mind, playing around the apartment while Galen was running extremely late errands for his boss. How the fuck was the man out of town and still needed Galen to wait on him hand and foot?

This promotion better be fucking good. If not, she'd have to march her ass up there, find this cock nugget boss of Galen's, and give him something to stress about.

Unless... what if he wasn't running errands for his boss?

What if he was cheating on her?

Her gaze narrowed as the thought occurred to her and threatened to disrupt reality.

"There's no way," she said aloud. Galen would *never* cheat on her. He worshiped the ground she walked on, had from day fucking one.

Between the two options, it was likely he was a fucking werewolf or some shit.

"Ugh!" she groaned and trudged to the computer. If nothing else, she could put her suspicions to rest and move on.

Her stomach twisted itself in a knot as she typed in a phrase. It felt so silly that she was actually asking Google for... she winced—a list of supernatural creatures and their habits.

She blamed the month of October, when they'd binged all the lame, cheesy horror movies they could find. It put too many ideas in her head.

The hits she got were overwhelming, press release after press release since the Big Reveal, but she spent the next few hours lost in the internet, wading through and narrowing down the list.

"He doesn't have an obsession with kissing my neck," she announced to the puppies.

Lissie tackled Bubba and took him to the floor, chomping on his ankles. He yelped out a playful bark and tried to twist and nip her ears.

"He doesn't disappear during the full moon. I haven't seen any spell books or weird symbols."

The list was dwindling fast. Nothing fit!

Her gaze latched onto a hyperlink at the bottom of the page, reading, "How to Deal with Others."

"Other what?" she grumbled, clicking the link loudly out of frustration.

When the page loaded, she scanned it and narrowed her eyes.

"How to protect against malevolent spirits and other supernatural beings. I'd say he's *other*, wouldn't you guys?"

The puppies ignored her.

Maeve clicked the link to the article, and the first thing she scrolled to was a list of five items that were effective against the supernatural.

"Okay, here we go," she murmured, scanning the article.

Her IQ felt lower after she read it. But more research didn't yield anything more promising, so after another hour of rabbit hole searches, she came back to her first tab.

"Fine. There's a little truth in every myth, or something like that, right?" she asked the pups.

They still didn't answer her, passed out after their latest romp. She was in this all alone.

"Salt?" she asked doubtfully, reading the first thing off the supernatural checklist.

She supposed she'd seen enough salt circles to know why it was supposed to work, but... "Whatever, let's just give it a shot, hmm?"

6. Salt to Taste

Maeve

"Here you go, sugar," she said, sliding Galen's plate in front of him once he'd settled in after returning from his errands for the day. "How was your day?" she asked.

Galen was none the wiser as he took the plate from her and centered it on his placemat. Little did he know... this was his first test.

"It was eh," he said, looking a little down even after their great start to the day. It almost made her feel guilty.

"Wanna talk about it?" she offered, stabbing her first potato with her fork. Maeve took a bite while eyeing Galen's plate. Almost.

Come on...

He lifted his gaze to her, and she snapped to attention. "Is it okay if I say not right now? You tell me about your day, that'll cheer me up."

Well, she certainly couldn't tell him she'd been researching how to repel him, could she?

"While you were gone, I was lazy," she admitted. "I laid around with the puppies." Not technically a lie. "Read a new book." It was articles instead of books, close enough. "Pretty boring to be honest."

Galen rested his cheek on his fist and sighed. "That sounds wonderful to me."

Maeve parted her lips, comforting words on the tip of her tongue, only to see Galen finally spear a potato as well.

She played it cool while he bit it off the fork, chewed for a moment, and swallowed. Trying to hide a wince, he washed it down with a sip of beer. It clicked to the table a moment later, and he cleared his throat. "It's a little... uh..."

"Delicious? Super awesome? The best meal you've ever had?" she suggested, staring at him innocently.

Salty as fuck because I used half the shaker? she thought to herself.

His lips twitched as he studied her before nodding. "Of course, sugar pie. It's amazing."

Much to Maeve's surprise, he finished the whole meal. Extra triple salt included. And he didn't even blink.

Not while eating, not while chugging water after the whole thing. Not even when he helped clear the table and wiped down the counter, including the salt she'd spilled by 'accident.'

What the fuck? She grumbled as she put the dry dishes away, Galen long gone to the bedroom after he washed. He'd been so dead on his feet she'd bumped him out of the way and taken over the drying. It was the least she could do after she'd clogged his arteries.

And of course she was using her alone time to the best of her abilities, pulling up the website from earlier and scanning it again.

I thought salt was supposed to repel him.

But he ate without blinking. Shouldn't it have burned or something?

The article had no further information of use to her, and she closed the tab with a sigh.

If that hadn't worked, surely something else on the list would.

Maeve would just have to learn it the hard way: trial by fire.

Silver.

She was sure the website meant something more literal. Like trying to stab him with a silver stake.

But I mean, if you stab anyone it's going to hurt.

It took her exactly three seconds to figure out how to discreetly expose Galen to silver without maiming him.

Pulling up an online retailer, she added a brand-new set of jewelry she'd been eyeing to the cart and checked out all within a few minutes.

Feeling proud, she laid her phone face down on the counter and sat her head in her hands.

Her elation lasted all of three seconds.

Now the only thing she could do was wait. And waiting was not something Maeve did well.

Should she go ahead with something else on the list? She hadn't read anywhere that she had to go in order.

Tapping her nails on the desk at work, she wavered back and forth. What did she have to lose?

Fuck it, she was making her own rules. Maeve would have to try iron.

After returning from another day of hell filled with endless phone calls and dumb questions from the population, she made dinner again like the excellent girlfriend she was.

"Cornbread?" Galen asked as he appeared behind her. He smelled clean from his shower, wrapping his arms around her as she stirred a small portion of soup.

"I was feeling soupy today," she said. "But not crackers. So cornbread it is."

The fact that the cornbread was now cooling in a cast iron skillet had absolutely nothing to do with her dinner menu.

"Sounds great to me. Thanks for cooking again, but I wouldn't have minded, just so you know."

She smiled. "Trying out for the job of househusband, huh?"

"If you'd give me a chance," he teased, leaning down to nip her shoulder.

It sent chills over her skin, and she shivered then wiggled away from his embrace. "No more touchy. You can set the table for me," she suggested, bumping her hip against him playfully.

Galen groaned, but finally released her and trailed to the cabinets to do as requested.

It made her frown as she stirred the soup, the many vegetables spinning and swirling in the broth. Galen was a good guy and a better boyfriend. The stuff they talked about *was* already improving. Each day another little bud of hope bloomed, and with it, trust in what he'd promised her.

Indecision swirled in her stomach. Galen was good to her. Should she even be putting him through these dumb trials?

But what if?

What if something *was* wrong? And what if it was something as extreme as... as being another species? She couldn't ignore *that*.

Vampire? Werewolf? Fae? Something? She wasn't very well versed in her supernatural beings. Maybe she should have paid more attention during the Big Reveal.

How could they go any further if he was keeping secrets from her? Maeve didn't like secrets. She didn't like the fact that Galen was keeping something from her. And she was nosy enough to gather her own intel and find out what.

Maybe it would be nothing, and they could laugh about all this in five years.

Mind made up, she swirled the soup one more time before shutting the burner off and grabbing her pot holders.

Transferring the pot to the table, she placed it on the oven mitt and began to scoop them a steamy serving.

"Will you grab the cornbread? It's cool enough now."

As she spooned them each some vegetable soup, she kept an eye on Galen. From the corner of her eye, she watched him approach the counter where she'd been cooling the cornbread. When he extended his arm to grab the pan, she held her breath, cranking her neck around to see him better. She had a clear view of him grabbing the cast iron skillet by the handle and—

Simply turning and bringing it to the table. Barehanded. With no reaction.

"What?" he asked, catching her gaze.

She said the first thing that came to mind. "Nothing. Just checking out your ass."

The way Galen's lips curled made her belly warm, so she averted her gaze and finished filling their bowls. Galen got them each a slice of cornbread, and they ate like... normal. Like they did every other night, before she ever suspected anything weird.

It was almost enough for her to doubt herself, to call the whole thing off. But she didn't. She'd started this for a reason, and she was going to see it through.

But it definitely didn't feel like she was sitting across the table from some kind of... supernatural creature.

Then again, he'd been fooling her for an entire year. This *was* normal for him.

That made her bitter all over again, but she still ate dinner with a smile. With jokes and laughter. It made it difficult to figure out where the line was.

She couldn't watch Galen's expression soften every time he looked at her and still try to tell herself that he was something... else.

Maeve was just going to have to prove it to herself.

Maeve discovered something about Galen during her investigation.

How had she never realized it before? Galen was hot as hell, with dark hair and a genuine smile and nice pecs and nicer muscles and an ass you could take a bite out of—*okay, we get it.*

Her boyfriend was hot.

But he was very clueless.

Galen never questioned her, or as far as she could tell, even suspected anything was weird.

He's dating you *so maybe his threshold for weirdness has changed.*

Rolling her eyes at herself, Maeve pushed the thoughts aside and stretched her arms up. "Here," she called up. A second later, Galen's voice echoed down the foldout ladder from the attic, accompanied by a cardboard box. She caught it with an *oof* and an explosion of dust.

She sneezed and turned around to set the box down.

Yes, this *was another* test for Galen. She was still awaiting the jewelry, so she'd skipped ahead to the last suggestion—religious relics.

If any of these crazy ideas were going to work, it would be this one. Don't ask her why. Maybe it was the remnants of her grandmother's religious teachings, some of which happened to be stored in this big box.

And if it did work... well. Maeve hadn't thought that far ahead.

Galen climbed down from the attic with a snuffle and a sneeze. "You know," he said as he found his footing on the ladder, "when we agreed to downsize our things so we could move in together, I meant like, some of the fifty pairs of shoes you own. Not family heirlooms stored in the attic."

"Hey, it's still getting rid of stuff, isn't it?" she called over her shoulder. His steps grew closer as he made his way down the ladder. The springs squeaked with each step, but he'd assured her they were sturdy. So if he fell from the ceiling, it wasn't her fault.

Still, she breathed a sigh of relief as he began to fold the ladder up with a clatter of wood and screech of old metal.

"What's in here anyway?" he asked, coming up behind her to look over her shoulder.

"Let's find out," she answered and opened the cardboard flaps.

First—lots of newspaper. That was all she saw at first, until she realized the newspaper was wrapped around fragile items. Porcelain baby dolls, a nativity scene.

"Oh, look! It's my first bible," she exclaimed. She pulled the baby blue book out, shimmery lined pages faded with age. Maeve handed it over to Galen who didn't hesitate to take it from her, even flipping through the pages. No reaction.

Hmm.

"I thought you were an atheist?" he asked.

"I am. I was raised in the church though," she explained. "To be honest I don't remember a whole lot about the experience itself. Just stories the pastors and stuff would tell us. Oh, look!" she said, pulling out a cross that had hung in her grandmother's living room throughout her whole childhood. She explained it to Galen as she ran a finger down the smooth wood. "Wow, I haven't seen this in years."

Leaning over, she held it out to him and pointed out a chip in the top corner. "I'm responsible for that," she confessed.

Galen gasped dramatically. "What?! You heathen!"

Maeve couldn't help her laugh. "That's exactly what my grandmother said, before I had to scrub the bathroom tile with a toothbrush."

He winced. "Oof."

"Yeah..." Maeve shook her head and handed the item over. If anything, *this* relic would have the strongest emotional attachment to her. Which would make it more powerful, according to the website.

Time seemed to slow down as Galen reached out for it, long fingers extending innocently. Maeve held her breath as she held it out to him. His fingertips brushed it... and then he wrapped his hand around it and took it from her grip.

"It's pretty," he remarked before setting it down.

Maeve must have been looking at him weird. "What? You okay?"

She shook her head. "Yeah! Just thinking about...uh, her. Grandma," she lied.

Sorry, Grandma.

Frustration laced through her. Galen was either an actor worthy of an Oscar, or—

Or there wasn't *anything* wrong with him, and she just pushed her own emotional baggage onto him, which in turn would only create more trauma and damage their relationship—

Stop it!

Maeve released a sigh and halfheartedly unpacked the rest of the box.

And then Galen made her go through her shoes, which was offensive enough. Maybe she should just end things now.

Honestly.

"They are *both* black, short booties! Why do you need two pairs?" Galen asked.

"Because! One is leather and one is suede. They both send two very different messages."

"Oh my god," Galen said, exasperated, crossing his arms and dropping his head into one hand.

"Oh my god," Maeve mimicked.

Galen lifted his head, arching a brow in that *way* he had that made her aware of the thin edge she was walking. "You better watch it, or I'll have you repeating that properly."

Never one to follow warnings, Maeve carried on. "Oh, there's a proper way?"

Galen snuck up behind her, wrapping his arms around her waist and kissing her neck.

Not a vampire, she chided herself.

"I'll have to remind you." But then he released her, chuckling at her disappointed expression. "Eventually."

7. Accessorize

Maeve

Her jewelry arrived a few days later. Unlocking her box and finding the discreet packaging, she couldn't hide her smile. Then it was a race back up the stairs to their apartment. She fed the puppies in record time and locked herself in the master bathroom to try it on.

It took a little time, but she eventually wiggled the new bars and the shiny hearts in place. By the time she had the matching chain attached and the fancy lingerie to go with it, Galen was calling her name and coming through the front door.

"I'm home!"

Perfect timing.

She raced out to the bedroom door and cracked it open, giddy at the feel of the chain slipping against her skin. "I already fed the puppies, babe. I'm in the bedroom."

Maybe it was the tone of her voice, the hint of excitement she just couldn't hide. She heard his bag drop instantly, followed by pounding steps through the apartment.

With a chuckle, she skipped to the bed and situated herself beneath the covers, barely pulling it up to her chin to hide her surprise by the time he—

Galen threw open the door, gaze latching onto her, expression shifting into one of adorably surprised excitement. "What's this?" he asked, somehow managing to keep his voice all low and rumbly.

The last test.

"A surprise. Assuming you shower fast enough to enjoy it."

Galen walked to the bathroom, keeping his gaze on hers, even going so far as to walk into the bathroom backwards. His waggling eyebrows had her in stitches by the time the door closed.

There was no way Galen was anything supernatural. Could a vampire make her laugh this hard? Weren't they supposed to be dead anyway? Undead? Something.

Apparently, pondering the supernatural took plenty of time, or Galen showered at the speed of light, because then he was opening the bathroom door in a cloud of steam.

"So is it my birthday?" he asked with a half smile, towel unfortunately wrapped around his waist.

"Nope."

"Not our anniversary. Not my promotion. Did *you* get a promotion?" he mused as he slowly stalked toward the bed.

"Nope. I just... wanted to buy something pretty for myself."

"And something I can enjoy too? How generous of you." His voice got lower and lower until he stopped at the bedside.

He leaned over and planted both palms beside her head, making her bounce in place. Pleasantly startled, she gasped, a smile already curling her lips.

Galen was looking downright predatory, and she'd never been more happy to be prey—

No. What are you saying? Maeve didn't know if he wasn't... if he was something other. She couldn't give in yet.

But his gaze was so dark and intense, and she was turning to a puddle the longer he stared at her, unwavering.

Ugh.

Let's be real.

She'd been wet ever since she changed her piercings. Imagining his reaction, wondering what he'd do when he saw them.

Galen's hand twitched on the mattress, and then white filled her vision as she gasped.

"Oosh!" she complained, and then pouted as the sheet fluttered to her feet. "Galen," she whined. "I wanted to do the big reveal."

"None needed," he said, eyes firmly locked on her own. "You're stunning enough."

His heated gaze trailed over her like a tangible caress, warm and hopelessly obsessive as he lingered over her figure.

Oh, *that* was what made her blush?

"I wanna touch you," he breathed, dark eyes glimmering as he crawled over her on the bed. Despite his words, almost a plea—*that* wouldn't be on repeat in her mind for the next week—their skin didn't so much as brush as he carefully balanced himself above her.

"You're like a goddamned dream," he mused as his gaze drifted to her face, lingering on her lips for just a second more.

Lying still beneath him, she waited for Galen to come to her.

And he did, just like she knew he always would, head lowering to hers with something close to awe in his expression.

It was a sweet kiss, golden honey dripped onto her lips. With a sweet tooth like hers, she couldn't help but brush her tongue out for a taste.

His mouth actually wavered against hers, breath shuddering out to spill across her cheeks before he swallowed the distance between them.

Their mouths were the only point of contact between their bodies, a bridge between two entire continents—or at least, that was how she felt, shivering from the desire. If only he'd touch her.

But Maeve wanted him to want her enough to endure the awkwardness of asking permission.

She loved when Galen asked permission.

So she kissed him and fisted her hands in the sheet to keep from reaching for him. When the kiss finally broke in exchange for a breath, Galen groaned.

"Fuck, look at you." His gaze traced her features, the line of her throat, lower. "I have to touch you. Please let me touch you," he whispered.

His hand was already lifting from beside her head as she nodded.

And because Galen was wonderfully, absolutely in love with her, the first thing he did was cup the back of her neck, fingers sliding through dark locks and thumb brushing over her jaw. He tilted her head up, and she let him pull her to him, lips brushing hers in nothing more than a caress. A taste, his soft hum rumbling against her lips, and finally, he crushed their lips together.

His thumb stroked her cheek in the softest of touches, while their lips melted together. It dissolved into messy, desperate need as she nipped his lip, and he slid his tongue between hers. She unclenched her hands from the sheets and stroked her fingers over the strong line of his shoulders, tugging at him.

Galen stubbornly refused to let himself fall atop her like she wanted. He could crush her into the mattress, and she'd say *thank you*, a plea dripping from her lips. An idea struck her, and she grinned into the kiss as she trailed a hand off his shoulder, down the front of his body, his pecs and flat, strong stomach, until the rough material of the towel brushed her fingertips.

She located the fold at his hips and wiggled her fingers on the other side of it before unraveling it with a gentle tug. *Success*, she thought as the fabric fell open, and she tugged it off, dropping it along the side of the bed without a second thought. As soon as her hand was free, she placed it back on his hip, tracing the long line of his side, back to his shoulders.

Galen's skin was especially warm from the shower, and she sighed, breath sliding past their lips as she traced and touched every part of him—chastely. So caught up in him, the beauty of him and knowing he was *hers* that she almost forgot *she* was to be *his* surprise.

"Trying to steal my thunder?" he teased once he parted the kiss.

"Can't help it. You look so good in... nothing."

"You're one to talk. Fuck, just look at you," he murmured.

"You can do more than look," she hinted, and maybe it was the soft tone of her voice that snapped him out of it.

He finally let his weight fall onto her, and she shivered as his warm skin finally met hers, thigh to chest, and then lips again as he took her mouth. He pressed her into the bed, and she couldn't so much as rock against the thigh pressed between hers.

She loved it, loved how he made her hold back so he could take his time.

Maeve tilted her head up to him, feeding into the kiss with every ounce of desire that flooded her. His fingers carefully unthreaded from her hair, and she found herself holding her breath as his touch drifted along her collarbones before sliding lower.

"Can I?" he whispered into the kiss, fingers hovering above her breast and the attached chain, warm from the press of their skin.

"Fuck, finally—" Her breath exploded out of her as Galen gently twitched his finger on the thin, one hundred percent silver chain attached at each end to the heart piercings in both nipples. A jolt of arousal pinged between the slight pull to the pulsing need in her core.

He paused, dark eyes still locked on hers, surveying her reaction. "Good?"

Maeve barely registered that he didn't get hurt from the chain.

So... not a vampire, right? Or was it werewolves that were supposed to react to silver?

In that moment, Maeve couldn't remember, and with Galen staring down at her so dark and delicious and wanting, she didn't want to.

"Good," she breathed. Reaching up, she fisted her hand in Galen's dark, wet curls and tugged him down to her. "Very good," she repeated before crushing their lips together.

Galen tasted her lips, just a tease, before he was sliding his lips lower, over her jaw. Maeve tilted her head up, giving him more room without even having to think about it. His smile branded her skin as he nipped and kissed and teased bruises into her throat before ever deciding to move lower.

"I've got work tomorrow, y'know," she warned, though it came out breathless and totally defeated the purpose of the warning at all.

His hum didn't seem very concerned.

"It's too warm for turtlenecks," she continued, but arched her neck more as he teased right under her ear.

"Wear a scarf or something," he mumbled between kisses.

Maeve couldn't hide the smile curling her lips, the absolute delight that burst in her chest. "Still too warm."

"A cravat," he suggested.

Maeve pretended to think it over with a hum. "I don't have an outfit that warrants one."

"I'll buy you one," he answered, finally drifting lower to her collarbones.

"I could just wear them proudly," she whispered with a knowing little grin.

He stiffened against her, thigh brushing between her legs, and she jolted at the contact. Then he continued, dipping lower across her chest, lips leading the way as he hummed against her. "I find that option most favorable," he rumbled, words spilling across her skin.

Maeve heaved a breath as his hand cupped her waist, sliding up to brush his thumb along the underside of her breast. Chills rippled across her skin, tightening her nipples and making her shiver beneath him.

Galen paused, lips poised over her hard, pink, jewel-tipped breast, gaze lifting to hers.

It was completely unfair for Galen to take her breath away like this, totally against the rules for him to look at her like that, eyes all wide and dark and wanting, desire shining from their depths like so many stars.

Before she could part her lips with a plea on her tongue, he lowered his head.

She shook at the hot drag of his tongue across the piercing. He traced around it, stopping to suck the chain between his lips and tug. Her back arched as she chased him for more, but he followed the chain instead, sprinkling chaste kisses along her sternum. Her nails tightened over his shoulders, combing through his hair to hold him against her.

"Love these," he murmured hotly across her skin. "Best purchase you ever made."

"You said that about the lingerie last time too," she mused, though her breath caught as he nipped her skin.

"You have excellent taste," he quipped, lips dragging across her skin in the hottest way.

Maeve couldn't think of a retort, though he pushed a loud moan out of her mouth as he tugged at the chain again, pinched between his teeth.

Her fingers tightened in his hair as he stopped, drew her gaze with his hesitation, and she glanced down to find it wasn't hesitation at all that stopped him in his path. He gazed up at her with a smirk curling those full lips. "Good?" he asked. "Sounded good."

"Good," she agreed, and tried to pull his mouth back to her. "Very good."

Galen let her lead him back down to her chest, and he pulled a whine from her as he wrapped his lips around the pink tip, jewelry and all. He swiped his tongue over the peak, sending addictive, electric pulses straight to her core.

She shivered beneath him as he dragged moans and pleas from her, until he mouthed across her skin to her other breast and repeated it all over again

She curled her right knee up around his hip, grinding into the thigh between her legs with a moan. "Galen," she pleaded.

His length was hard and thick against her, and she tried to press her thigh up into him, but he arched his hips away. Maeve grunted out her disappointment, felt his lips curl into a grin against her skin.

"How do you want it?" he asked, lips brushing against her nipple with every word. Warmth bloomed in her core, and she shifted against him in a miniscule movement, unable to find the words, just that she wanted *more*.

He hummed, kissing lower on her chest, dipping toward her belly. "You could come on my tongue like the other day." His voice was like melted sugar, thick and sweet, and it made her thoughts slow and sticky as she was overcome with the memory he described. "Love watching you shake beneath me. And I bet..." He paused, pressing a kiss to her stomach. "The chain would shimmer so prettily as you did so."

Her body was listening to him more than she was, and a shiver danced up her spine, making her shake beneath him just like he described. His swallow was audible, endearing the moment.

"Yep," he rasped out. "It shimmers. Fuck."

As she rolled her hips up into him, she groaned, fingers tightening in his hair to bring him all the way back up to her lips. He studied her, gaze passing over hers briefly, enough for her to see the desire bright in his dark eyes.

"I want you inside me," she whispered across his lips.

His hand twitched in the sheets near her head, and she resisted the taste of a smile on her lips.

She shoved at his shoulder, and his heated expression cracked into one of surprise as he let himself be pushed over. He landed on his back, and Maeve followed him, throwing a leg over his hip and settling atop him with a triumphant smile. Settled atop his hips, she ground down into him, over the hard length of his cock resting against his stomach. It punched the breath from his chest, and she reveled in the sound, at the proof of how much she affected him.

The grind was slick and easy as she rolled her hips over him, so wet from his teasing and his kisses and all his soft, slutty promises.

His hands spread warmth over her skin as he skimmed them over her thighs, around her hips and up her torso before cupping her breasts. Arching into the touch, she bit her lip as she pushed her taut, achy nipples into his palms.

As his thumbs pressed over the tips and teased the jewelry, tugged at the chain, he lifted the other hand to her lip, tugging it out of the grip of her teeth.

"Wanna hear you," he explained, and she let her eyes fall closed as she sucked in a breath too big for her chest.

Fuck.

Maeve hummed, the sound shaky as she lifted up, wrapped a hand around his cock, and notched him at her core.

"Now," she whispered. "Want you now."

Matching groans punched the air as she let gravity do the work, sliding herself down on him in a short, needy motion. She was warm all over, inside and out, heat flushing her cheeks and chest and core. She sat up once again, stopping when he was still *just* inside her before sinking back down, all the way, until she sat atop his hips.

Her knees were already shaky, and she nudged her hips over him, adjusting to the stretch of him inside her. But she couldn't wait long, found herself pressing into her knees and moaning at the drag of him inside her before she reversed, letting him slowly fill her again.

Shivers of pleasure danced across her senses, down her spine, and melted in her core as he plucked and brushed his thumbs over her nipples and lightly tugged at the chain until moans were pouring from her lips. Her hips moved faster, chasing more, letting him fill her again and again.

"Fuck, look at you," he rasped. "So fucking *pretty* like this."

Maeve's fingers twitched, digging into his chest at the awe, praise, and admiration dripping from his lips. She slowed the pace, hips moving slow and syrupy as she tightened around him.

His eyes fluttered shut, head falling back onto the bed as he groaned, the sound welling from so deep inside him she felt it beneath her palms.

Galen melted right before her eyes, and a fresh kick of heat landed in her stomach, punctuated by the grind of hips, the thrust of his cock inside her. His praises never failed to inspire warmth, but Maeve was more often than not struck entirely dumb by how... magnetic Galen was.

Like now, with his neck arched back, curls crushed into the mattress and lips parted. Chest both tense and plush beneath her fingers, his hips grinding up into her every movement, hands gripped around her waist and forearms veined in his control.

"Look at you," she moaned. "Hot, you're so hot."

Okay, so maybe not the most creative words, the prettiest prose, but her brain couldn't come up with much else. Not with him coming apart beneath her and moaning her name and snapping his hips up to bounce her against him. He planted his feet behind her, pulling his knees up and shifting the angle.

Maeve gasped and leaned into him, her arm coming to rest atop his knee, giving her more leverage, knocking the breath from her lungs with the new angle, stars sparkling across her vision in the brilliance of pleasure.

"Shit, Maeve—fuck," he rumbled, and together they increased the pace. His hands on her hips dragged her back down onto him once she sat up, cunt clenching around him on each thrust.

A push and a pull, back and forth, they crashed together again and again in a collision of bodies and pleasure and need.

"You look so fucking good like this," Galen murmured, eyes dark and heavy and half-lidded as he gazed up at her. "A work of art, a goddamned masterpiece."

The adoration in his words made her chest expand, warm and tight with overwhelming fondness, and all at once their connection was so bright and brilliant she could only moan.

Could only let her body say the words she couldn't manage to string together, vampire or werewolf or *other* be damned. Because *that* was more likely than him spoiling what they had by looking elsewhere, because everything he wanted was right here and she knew it. From the way his hands grasped at her like he couldn't bring her close enough, the way his gaze sharpened briefly as he adjusted the position to pull another moan from her, to make her feel good, better, more amazing and glowing than she'd ever felt with another person in her entire life.

It swelled and pulsed between them, the ecstasy, the pleasure, and the want and need and of course the love too, but she wasn't chasing *love* with each bounce of her hips, because she didn't have to, she already had it. Tucked away in her chest cavity with his name stitched across the front.

"Galen." His name escaped on a breath, and she didn't know whether it was supposed to be a plea or a praise, and in the end, it didn't matter, because his deft fingers pinched the chain between two fingers and simply—pulled.

She shattered, cunt quivering around him as her head fell back, eyes closing against the burst of light behind her lids as pleasure scattered her senses, ruined the pace until it was a sloppy, messy tangle of limbs that rocked her back and forth on him until—

Until Galen moaned with his whole chest, hips stuttering beneath her, cock pulsing inside her as he came. Spilled inside her in a hot flood as the aftershocks still turned her inside out.

When it was quiet, once they'd caught their breath, once Maeve's heart wasn't racing in her chest anymore but simply keeping pace with the strong beat beneath her cheek, she... laughed.

A snicker burst free before it sparked into giggles, and she covered her mouth, turning her head into Galen's chest.

His chest expanded beneath her before the deep rumble of a chuckle sounded. He drew his hand to hers and pulled it away from her lips, and she tilted her head up at him, found his lips curled wide in a grin as he laughed with her. Maeve's chest was so full with adoration and tight with affection, and she didn't *know* she could love someone so absolutely.

"God, I love you," Galen said suddenly, the words exploded on a breath.

All it took was a glance to know that his thoughts mirrored her own, gaze heavy and bright with the same mixture of emotions that bumbled around in her own head.

"I love you too," she sighed.

8. Telling Shadows

Maeve

The next day, Maeve sighed and relaxed in the bathtub, letting the hot water steam up the bathroom. This was her treat for working so hard to prove her boyfriend was a vampire or something. But the real reason she was celebrating was because she hadn't found anything.

Galen didn't care how much salt she poisoned him with. He hadn't reacted to the cast iron skillet at all. And the churchy stuff she'd gotten down from the attic to go through? Galen didn't mind getting right there with her and helping her organize it.

She could also say the silver body jewelry had been a success. In more ways than one.

So no. Nothing had worked.

Galen was... normal.

Just a guy.

A smile curled her lips. *My guy.*

The longer she stayed in the bath, and the deeper she sank into the water, the less she cared about any of it. She was just happy things were okay. The promotion was just stressing him out, and he was probably not processing it well and acting weird as a result and everything would settle down after he received it. There was no need for her to be worried all this time.

A chuckle drifted out. She felt a little silly, to think she'd really gone through so much just to investigate her boyfriend's *humanity*.

Now, she had nothing to worry about.

Maeve let the light purple water drift over her skin. Lavender always cleared her head.

Once the water began cooling, she decided she'd pampered herself enough. When she opened the door and released all the steam, walking into the chilly air of the bedroom, she felt... refreshed, revived.

And finding Galen on the bed was the best sight ever.

"You're home!" she said, tucking her towel to keep it from slipping.

Galen turned his head to her, gaze trailing from head to toe. The heat in his gaze burned the closer she got, and when the tops of her thighs bumped the side of the bed, she looked down and found Galen staring up at her with a kind of wonder.

"The boss let me go early," he said with a sigh.

Maeve frowned. "You sound bummed. What's wrong?"

She tightened the towel and sat on the edge of the bed.

Not that it mattered, because if Maeve had anything to do with it, she wouldn't be wearing it for long.

"I'm just tired. I can see the light at the end of the tunnel. He *has* to make a decision by next week. So I'll know soon enough if all this bullshit has paid off."

Maeve hated the dull tone in his voice.

"I just... really, really want this promotion." Galen dug his palms into his eyes. "It pisses me off that I won't know until after I get done doing all his bidding. And if it ends up being for nothing..."

"That won't happen," she assured him, bumping his hands out of the way and smoothing her thumb over his chronically knotted brows. "I can't imagine anyone else working more diligently or being more dedicated to this promotion. You'll get it."

"You sound so sure," he said, tilting his head back to see her better. It elongated his neck, and she had the intrusive urge to chomp.

No. Now is not the time.

"I *am* sure." Maeve instilled all her belief in the three words. Galen was going to get this promotion. Did she understand why he wanted it so badly? Not really, but Galen had been gunning for it since they'd begun dating. It was only recently that the competition had gotten serious.

His frown relaxed, and he looked up at her with an expression she couldn't quite place.

"You're too good to me," Galen said. "I'm a lucky, lucky guy."

Her cheeks heated. "Stop it," she teased. "It was only like two weeks ago that I chewed you out."

"I needed it," he retorted. "I was slacking. You're not my mother, you shouldn't have to pick up after me."

She smiled. "Well, good to know you can distinguish me from your mother," she drawled.

"Hah, funny," he said without a hint of a laugh.

"You've been really stressed," Maeve told him, petting his hair. Maybe she should have taken that into account before giving him a hard time about the cleaning thing.

He nodded before pulling back and lifting his face up to her. "Yeah, it's been shitty," he admitted, letting his eyes drift closed.

Her lips tilted up at him. She couldn't help it. Sometimes he was just so... soft. And she was the only one who got to see him like that.

"De-stressing would be nice," he said, blinking one eye up at her.

With a skip, her heart tripped over itself to beat faster, but she smoothed out her expression. "Oh?" she encouraged.

"Yeah. But I mean, how could I?" He sighed dramatically. "If only there was a person, one special person, that knew just how to help—"

"Oh shut up, I get it," she interrupted, and lowered her head to kiss him.

At first it was upside down and clumsy and endearing altogether.

With a chuckle, she undid her tie on the towel and crawled down the bed until she could straddle him.

His lips were soft against hers, but the shadow of his beard always tickled her cheeks. It was a dichotomy she would never get tired of.

Maeve framed his square jaw with her palms and scratched her nails over the prickly stubble. His lips parted for her, and she tasted every inch of him until they were both panting, both sharing the same breath to fan the spark of flames between them.

Galen was still fully dressed, and she felt the press of him directly between her legs.

She paused, lips barely touching. She just wanted to hear the way Galen's breath quickened alongside hers, brushed across her cheek in a hot puff.

With one last peck to his lips, she trailed her kisses along his jaw, nipping and teasing along the way. When she got to his neck, she paused for a split second to check in. "Stoplight system?"

"Ooh are you gonna get mean?" he asked, sounding far too thrilled.

Maeve couldn't hide her smile. "Aren't I always?"

His smirk was dangerous, and he knew it. "The stoplight system is fine."

Satisfied they were on the same page, Maeve lowered her head so she didn't give into that smirk. She couldn't reveal how much he affected her, at least not when they were playing. Maeve would never hear the end of it.

She felt powerful with Galen, especially in this moment. Completely nude with him beneath her, yet he was waiting for her signal, waiting to hear what she wanted him to do. How she wanted him to please her.

It sent shivers down her spine, and she nipped what she knew was a sensitive spot for him, and he cursed.

"Long overdue," he murmured. "This is gonna be so good," he told her with a gasp.

"If you only knew how much trouble you're in," she whispered against his skin.

His fingers tightened around her hips, and she already felt the simmer of arousal in her belly.

"No touching," she told him.

He hesitated for the smallest second but gave in, letting his hands fall limply to the side. Lifting up, she stared down at him, noting his expression, gauging how he was feeling.

Galen was staring up at her through half-lidded eyes darkened with want. Desire. The same desire she'd grown to recognize as special. Galen reserved it just for her.

Maeve was relieved. Relieved that he still had that same desire for her, relieved she hadn't found anything during her super official investigation. Relieved Galen was just her Galen, like always.

Hot and perfect and seeming pretty punishable for stressing her out. If he hadn't been so fucking weird about this promotion the whole time, she wouldn't have assumed he was a damned werewolf or something.

She rolled her hips on him and felt his hardness between her legs.

"Already?" she teased.

His head snapped up at her taunt, a retort on the tip of his lips. And she couldn't wait to suck that attitude right out of him.

She slid down the bed, clawing her fingers and gently dragging them down his chest over his shirt. He snapped his mouth shut at her movements, fingers twitching against the sheet in anticipation.

"We'll have to make sure you can last, I'm not looking for a quickie here."

He groaned, thumping his head back down to the bed. But when her fingers went to his belt, he was lifting his hips and shuffling to help her get them down his legs. Then all she had to do was pluck at his shirt before he leaned up to pull it over his head.

Only when he was lying still again did she let her gaze finally drop, found him hard and straining, slickness already glistening on the tip.

"Prop yourself up, you need a better view," Maeve directed.

Galen grabbed one of her pillows and tossed it beneath his head.

Now when she lowered herself slowly, Maeve could meet the heat in his gaze as she tasted the tip of him. She almost hated to admit it, but Galen tasted oddly better than any other guy she'd ever been with. Even though they'd been together for a year, she still couldn't quite figure out why, but holy shit did it make torturing him with her tongue a hell of a lot more fun.

And oh was she going to torture him. For stressing her out. For being weird. For bringing the puppies home.

The puppies who were being blissfully quiet in the living room. No barking, no yipping. Peace.

She sighed, her breath warm against his head.

"Hair," she said absently. Galen gathered her hair in one hand and held it out of her way, giving himself a better view in the process. Just like she wanted.

Galen had always been weak for this, which was what made it so fun.

His cock pulsed in her grip, and she hid a smirk by wrapping her lips around his head, cherishing the harsh curse that spilled from his mouth.

Unable to resist the temptation, Maeve released him and met his gaze, wrapping her fingers loosely around him. "Is that anyway to talk to someone sucking your dick?"

His glare almost made her laugh. She *loved* playing with him like this.

Galen obviously enjoyed it, and Maeve got to be in control. And mean, if she wanted.

With that in mind, she arched a brow and waited patiently. By patiently, she meant tightening her fingers around his cock slightly, just enough for him to feel the difference. Just enough to tease. Enough to let him know that the longer he made her wait, the longer *he* was going to have to wait.

A short grumble vibrated through his chest, and she released her hand and cupped it in the air by her ear. "What was that? Couldn't quite hear you."

Staring up at him from her position, she felt powerful. And happy. Endorphins must be rushing around, doing their job.

Her heart pounded when Galen rolled his eyes, but he ultimately whispered, "You feel good. Please continue."

He didn't sound nearly wrecked enough for Maeve.

"Just *good?*"

Maeve wrapped her hand around him again, lowering her head once more and taking him inside her mouth. His groan was wordless, so she couldn't chastise him again, but listening to him was just as hot. Through their relationship and experimentation, Maeve had learned just which things drove Galen crazy. What turned him into putty. What made him come the quickest.

Maeve deployed her tactics from the latter category. Squeezing her hand around him, *just* this side of uncomfortable, she lowered her mouth, opening her throat and taking him down until she met the back of her hand.

Her lashes fluttered closed as she reveled in the feeling of him inside her, even if it wasn't where she wanted him most. Galen was big, she was proud to announce, and taking him deep always gave her a little flutter of pride. And the way Galen petted her hair and moaned wordlessly?

Well that shit just tickled her pink.

But this wasn't a time for Galen to comfort and pet her. She wanted him to beg.

Eventually.

First, she wanted to make sure he could withstand the torture for as long as she wanted to have fun.

Dragging her mouth back up, she followed with her fist before twisting her grip at the top, pressing her tongue against the head. Galen's groan reverberated through his entire body, and the hand in her hair tightened. She'd correct him, but then she'd have to take her mouth off his cock, and it was just getting *fun*.

So she let it go for now, and began bobbing her head, hollowing her cheeks. She repeated the same motions. Every time she got to the top, she'd twist her hand and tongue his head until she was rewarded with a drop of precum on each go.

Galen was a babbling mess above her, one hand in the sheets and the other tangled in her hair. She hadn't given him permission to talk, but the sounds he was making were so sweet she didn't want to stop them. He was being good.

Galen groaned above her, arching his back. "Oh shit, I'm close—close, close, close, close..."

Maeve continued even after his warning, sucking him deeper and sending him over the edge. He spilled in her mouth, down her throat, and Galen was putty in her hands, shaped from pleasure by the time she released him.

Tugging her up his chest, he kissed her, plunging his tongue inside her mouth to taste himself. His chest heaved beneath her, heart pounding, each beat for her.

Flattening her palms against his pecs, she pulled away and stared down at Galen. His pupils were blown, blinks drowsy as he stared up at her in wordless awe.

"We're not done yet, big guy," she said with an arched brow. "Far from it."

His eyes widened at that, and he stroked a hand up the outside of her thigh. "Oh really now? What's my next punishment?"

Maeve leaned down to his ear, nipped his neck before telling him. "You're going to get hard again, and then I want you to fuck me so hard and long that I can't think straight."

Maeve lowered herself back, sitting on his lap. His cock twitched, a valiant effort to return from the dead, but Maeve sighed dramatically, shuffling back until she straddled his thighs.

Galen was already half hard again, which was impressive for any man.

Maeve stared down at him, and Galen's stomach jumped under her perusal. "Looks like you need some help," she suggested sweetly.

Galen groaned. "Can I touch you yet?"

"No," she said dryly. Tonight wasn't a night for ropes, so she was going to have to trust that Galen would behave.

"You're so mean," he said, voice low and rumbly and delicious.

"And you love it," she whispered, lifting her eyes to meet his gaze. Slowly, Maeve slid her hands from her own thighs, down to her knees before skimming over Galen's thighs. Gliding her fingers up gently, she disturbed his dark hair and watched goosebumps crawl over his skin.

She paused, palm flat on the right side of his pelvis, and watched his gaze as she inched closer to his not fast enough erection.

A shift of his gaze, a twitch of his lips, a nervous swallow. She was looking for any sign that he was already too sensitive, but he didn't even breathe until she lifted her hand.

"Spit on me," he said, the request coming out on a rasp, as if he'd surprised himself with it.

"Happily," Maeve obliged. Wrapping her hand around him anyway, she stood him up and tilted her head down, gathering the saliva in her mouth before pursing her lips and releasing it. It dripped right on the head of his cock, in the circle she made with her thumb and forefinger.

Excellent aim, if I do say so myself.

He'd probably been expecting something a little meaner, but she was wet and getting a little impatient. Using the slickness to make the glide smoother, she stroked him to a full erection.

"Ah—ah," Galen gasped, hips hitching down, trying to get away from her touch.

"Aw, sensitive?"

He nodded, mouth slack and gaze locked on where her hand squeezed him slowly.

"Is it too much? Guess you won't be able to fuck me then, huh? What good are you?" She pouted for good effect, easing forward and sliding him between her legs.

He sucked in a sharp breath when he felt how wet she was. *Fuck, this man.*

"Fuck me," he said.

"What's that?" she asked, tilting her head at him with a sly smile.

Galen let his head smack against the mattress. "Ugh! Just ride me! Please, for the love of—"

All Maeve was searching for was that one tiny little word. Please. That was all it took before she lifted up, notched him at her center, and started lowering herself.

Pulling Galen apart like this required so much trust and care and attention, but it was worth every second. And it was so, so hot to have a man like Galen under her. One who adored her and all her weird quirks and her not-so-controlled temperament, who made her coffee with little sticky notes and cute doodles. Who found a hundred ways to say *I love you*, not even one of them found in the dictionary.

Maeve loved this big, soft idiot. Might even go so far as to say she needed him.

She wanted him to *need* her. And it was never more apparent how much until he was begging for her.

Lowering herself down his length, she wasn't satisfied until her ass met the tops of his thighs. Maeve paused for a moment, let the pleasure melt through her veins and heat her blood to boiling. "Fucking hell," she moaned. "You talk about me being perfect, but nothing is better than the way you fill me up."

His fingers gripped the sheets as she talked, as she slowly rocked herself on his lap. Every inch of him was inside her, and she felt so full, so *good*.

Trying to keep her last two brain cells together, Maeve grabbed his hands off the sheets and led them to her hips. Focused on remembering that no matter how soft she was for him, Galen needed more from her.

"Now fuck me like you're actually good at it," she snapped, though the order was mostly extinguished from the high-pitched gasp she let out as Galen finally slid her up his length before slamming her back down on his cock.

Since his hands were busy, Maeve lifted her own to her nipples, wiggling her piercings and sending sparks of pleasure through her body. It all coalesced in her center, in the bundle of nerves that wasn't quite getting what she needed.

"Come on, I know you can do better than that," she taunted, though the sharpness of her tease was blunted by gritted teeth.

Galen stirred himself in her, holding her against him as he ground up against her.

"Oh my god," she gasped, voice high-pitched as she dropped her head, palms landing on either side of Galen.

"See? Told you I'd remind you," Galen said, but Maeve felt too good to give into his tease.

"You better not come before me," was all she could think of.

Galen's hips twitched at that.

Now that he had her permission, his fingers bruised her hips where he held her. Where he began to snap his hips up and drag her down onto him at the same time. His movements grinded her clit against him in a chaotic rhythm.

Finally, *this* was what she needed.

Galen was chasing his own pleasure, his strokes erratic and rushed, and his rasping breaths and moans were loud in her ear.

Turning her head to the side, she muffled her own whines against her skin.

Maeve felt Galen pulse inside her as his pace stuttered. He was close, and she was growing closer with every punch of his hips and every glide of him inside her.

With a growl, Galen pulled her hips to him and paused there, stilling them suddenly. She turned her head back to face him because, like, what the fuck?

Before she could even part her lips to ask, Galen rolled them to the side and situated them, flipping her over and grabbing her hips, pulling her ass up in the air. She arched for him, gripping the sheets tight as he slammed back inside and set a bruising pace that pushed the breath from her lungs with every thrust.

"Talk to me," he demanded.

Maeve swallowed, turning her head to the side so he could hear her.

"Have you not come yet?" she gasped out. The words probably would have sounded a little more scathing had she not been taking every inch of Galen's cock. "Exactly how much pampering do you think you deserve before you have another orgasm?" The words came out between muffled moans, but they had her desired effect.

With her head turned toward the side, she could barely see Galen out of the corner of her eye, but her attention was rapt on the movement of their shadows. With the moon streaming in, their shadows were cast across the floor, framed by the dim light. She dug her teeth into her lip, watching the shadows move in unison with each thrust.

He groaned, loud and long and as sounding as desperate as she felt, as his hips stuttered, as she fluttered around him in the first waves of an orgasm.

Maeve muffled her whine and gripped the covers so hard her knuckles turned white as pleasure flooded her.

"Fuck, fuck, fuck, I can feel you—" Galen panted.

Her eyes tried to drift closed, but she snapped them open, watching Galen's shadow shake. His hands squeezed her hips hard as he pulled her back onto him and held her there. She felt him jerk as he came, felt the shudder run through him and watched the shadow do the same.

She blinked, dazed in thrumming pleasure, and suddenly the shadows were... different. Blinking again, she studied Galen's. His stain on the floor changed. One split second it was him, and the next it... wasn't. Almost like it was distorted, except Maeve was certain the new shadow had horns and wings that didn't belong. Heart in her throat, she turned her head the other way, seeing the moon bright and solid directly through the clear window.

Galen sighed and encircled his arms around her stomach, leaning over her back to pepper her shoulders with kisses.

She turned her head back the other way, and the shadows were normal again. The curve to Galen's back was smooth, no wings jutting out.

Rolling over in his arms, she stared up at him, half expecting to see horns sticking out of his head. But his inky waves were the same as usual, if a little mussed from their activities.

A half smile curled her lips as she reached up to fluff it back into place. His hair had probably just fallen out of place, distorting the shadow.

"Hi," she said quietly, staring up at Galen.

The lines around his eyes were relaxed, his brows missing their usual knot.

"Hi," Galen echoed.

Maeve tugged him down to her and kissed him, running her hands through his hair softly. Then she pulled him down next to her. His massive frame bounced on the bed as he landed, and Maeve curled around him, head on his chest.

Her legs were still a little shaky, so she needed a moment to breathe. And Galen had been so good, he deserved a little rest too.

"Feel okay?" she asked him, rubbing her cheek against his pec.

"Better than okay," he answered with a sigh, his chest deflating beneath her. Galen caressed a pattern on her back. "Everything was so... awesome," he finally settled on, and Maeve couldn't help her chuckle.

"Hey, words are hard right now, okay? You just sucked the life out of my cock and then milked me dry. Cut a guy some slack."

Despite all the words she'd just said to him in the heat of the moment, her cheeks pinkened at his description.

"You're welcome," she retorted simply.

His chest shook as he laughed, the soft, deep rumble echoing around the room. Then they were both quiet, and Maeve was working up the energy to drag them both to the shower when Galen spoke again.

"I fuckin' love you, you know that?" he said, as if the words had been banging around his teeth until he let them out.

It made her heart squeeze, and she suddenly couldn't speak for the lump in her throat. Pressing into her palms, she lifted herself up to meet Galen's gaze.

"You're just so... I mean, at the risk of sounding like a total sap, you're pretty goddamn perfect." She watched his lips curl on every word, watched his eyes as they studied her face.

She parted her lips, wanting to return the sentiment, but she couldn't even put it into words. Galen was pretty fucking amazing too. What she finally decided on was, "I guess you make existing not suck so much. Living together isn't *so* bad."

At Galen's arched brow, she let a soft smile curl her lips, and she leaned up to let him taste it. "I love you too," she echoed.

9. Suspicions

Maeve

Eventually, they worked up the energy to make it to the shower. And then afterwards, when Galen's skin was all deliciously warm from the hot water?

It was a good thing Galen liked cuddling after they played, because Maeve did too. As they crawled in bed together, she made like a magnet and got comfy with him, soaking up his heat.

"I swear you like my chest more than your own pillow," he remarked.

"What is it you say?" Maeve asked sleepily. "'Boobs make the best pillows?'"

"I do not have boobs," Galen argued.

Maeve slid a hand up his abs until her palm cradled the shape of his pec. "I beg to differ."

It was quiet for so long Maeve wondered if he fell asleep. But then his shoulders shook. "Insufferable," he muttered, chest bouncing beneath her cheek.

"You love it," she retorted, and nipped his skin before kissing the sting away.

She fell asleep on his chest, with his arm around her back and a hand in her hair.

It was the deepest, most peaceful sleep she'd had in *days* when consciousness tried to interfere. Maeve batted it away with a groan and rolled over. Surely it wasn't morning yet!

But it wasn't the light of day that finally dispersed the hazy fog of sleep. It was the lack of warmth in the bed next to her.

Grumbling, she blinked her eyes open and let them adjust to the darkness before searching out the clock.

"Three thirteen? Come on," she muttered.

The bed was empty again, Galen's spot still cooling from his absence. Where'd he go now? Another bad dream?

As concern filled her chest, she sat up, swinging her legs over the side. It was chilly without the protection of the blankets, so she aimed for a pair of sweats, but the quiet click of a door closing made her pause.

Her heart skipped a beat as she shut the drawer and pulled open the bedroom door.

"Galen?" she called out quietly.

Silence answered her. She tugged the sweatpants up her legs in record time, and it only took a split second, a short glance around the apartment, to know that he was gone. The puppies snored in a pile in front of the couch, but no Galen.

"What the hell?" she asked aloud. Her gaze traveled to the window, the streetlamps beyond, and the darkness in between. A familiar build tucked away in a long-sleeved, dark tee passed under one of the lights.

Maeve narrowed her gaze before snapping out of it. "You're mine now," she bit out. Racing to the door, she stabbed her feet into her sneakers and grabbed her keys and jacket before shutting the door behind her and locking it.

Her mind raced with ideas as she hurried down the stairs and onto the sidewalk. With quick but quiet steps, she jogged in the direction she'd seen Galen go. There was a turn up ahead, and she slowed down as she approached, not wanting to give herself away.

She didn't see him straight ahead, so he must have taken the left. Glancing down the road, she spied his tall figure a few blocks ahead, and followed.

Her knees were still fucking weak from the way she'd made him fuck her, and yet here she was, stalking her boyfriend to see why the fuck he was leaving the house at three in the morning.

First investigating, now stalking?

No, it's like a stake out. You're gathering information.

"Yeah, that," she whispered.

Honestly, Maeve should have tried this whole detective thing earlier. Obviously, she was a natural, because now she *knew* something was up. There was no normal reason to be leaving the house secretly at three in the morning.

So maybe he wasn't a supernatural creature. But something was going on, and she damned well was going to find out what.

Galen was a couple yards ahead of her, pace hurried, but not rushed. The more she followed, the more she could make out about him. He had earbuds in, hands in his pockets like he was taking an evening stroll.

It was weird that he was wearing headphones in the middle of the night. Wouldn't he want to know if someone was coming up behind him? It was dangerous out here this time of night.

Unless... she blinked. Unless he was the thing to be afraid of in the dark?

A shiver danced up her spine and she shimmied it away and continued to slink on Galen's trail.

For the longest time, it was only streetlamps and the eerie sound of the quiet city. And Galen. It wasn't long before she began to wonder if she'd made it all up. Why was she even out here? Galen was clearly wandering around with no destination. Hell, maybe he liked to go on late night walks?

But why wouldn't he just tell me that?

Maeve huffed. Her subconscious had a good point.

So she kept on his trail, until he finally took a sharp right. But Maeve knew this area, knew that he'd taken a turn into an alley with no outlet. It was a dead end.

Nervous, her heart began thumping harder in her chest as she glued herself to the sides of the buildings and eased closer. Her steps were silent as she inched toward the alleyway.

She crouched to her knees and tried to calm her racing heart. The brick wall was rough against her hands as she splayed them out to keep her balance on her toes. It was cold, making her nose burn.

With a deep, painful breath, she peeked around the corner of the building into the alley.

And for a split second, Galen was just standing there, facing the back of the alley and breathing deeply. Confusion swirled in Maeve's chest. Why would he come all the way out here just to stare at a brick wall—

Galen's voice echoed around the alley, more words that she didn't recognize, couldn't comprehend. Goosebumps spread over her body, head to toe, and she shivered though it had nothing to do with the cold.

Heart racing, she stared at her boyfriend as he chanted more nonsense—just like he had with the puppies—before a soft glow filled the alley. At first, she only had to squint against it, but it got so bright so fast that she ducked back behind the brick corner to shield her eyes.

When it faded, she blinked her eyes open and slid back around the corner.

She froze.

In place of Galen stood... something. Something more. With... with wings.

Beneath the soft glow of them, she spied the remaining tatters of his black shirt.

Just like all the others.

The glow faded all together and all Maeve was left with was shock. She couldn't blink, afraid he would disappear, and she would convince herself it was all a dream.

But this was real. That was Galen. With wings and... horns.

Her heart skipped a beat as Galen stretched his neck out, and in the dull light from the streetlamp, his horns were visible.

Maeve was committing him to memory, from head to toe. Because she knew she wasn't crazy. He was right the—

In a puff of smoke, he was gone. The alley was empty.

Maeve stood, her hands moving up the wall as she steadied herself. Shaky steps took her into the alley, and wide eyes assessed the area. Was it a prank? There was no camera, no smoke machine, no tarp or special effects.

It was just brick and concrete and some trash.

Maeve's heart pounded in her chest. She felt it in her throat and in her head, until all she could hear was her blood rushing.

Sucking in a desperate breath, Maeve uncurled her hands from fists, unwound her fingers from her palms, leaving behind half-moons. The sting reminded her that yes, if it wasn't blatantly obvious, this was real.

Maeve ran.

She didn't care how crazy it made her look, didn't care how many people saw her or how many times she tripped over the sidewalk as she raced back home.

The familiarity of her apartment complex made her chest ache, or maybe that was just her lungs burning for air.

She raced up the steps and yanked her key out before she got to the door. Glancing over her shoulder, she half expected Galen to be following behind her, but the hallway was empty, silent except for the breath rushing past her lips.

Her hand was shaking, and the key wouldn't go in the fucking lock, and she felt like someone was just right behind her and—the knob turned as the key did its job, and she pushed in the door, slamming it shut behind her.

Skittering claws sounded throughout the apartment, and she yelped as the puppies came racing toward her. She must have startled them awake when she left.

"Oh my god," she breathed, the image of wings bursting from Galen's shirt was burned into her mind. So that made him what? Some kind of... "Demon? A devil? What else has wings?" she asked aloud.

The puppies yelped and skidded to a stop near her at the same time the revelation did, and she jumped away from them.

"Don't touch me!" she yelled, sprinting for the kitchen island.

A demon. Three dogs. Three black dogs.

She splayed out on top of the counter in an enviable display of grace before getting to her knees on the hard marble and staring toward the doorway.

A dozen paws skittered and three pink tongues flopped from their mouths as they raced after her. Just like they did when it was play time. But her heart was beating against her chest, and playfulness was the last emotion from her mind.

"You're not even real puppies," she cried out as they circled the kitchen table.

They were probably some kind of demon dog! Why else would he have three puppies?

There was one in Greek mythology she'd learned about in high school, but god, that was so long ago, and she couldn't remember it right then. Not when their little teeth and big brown eyes—

Red eyes scored her vision.

"You fuckers!" she shouted. "I'm not crazy! You do have glowing eyes!" She pointed down at the pups who were jumping at the kitchen island, as if they had any idea what she was saying.

Maeve had to admit she felt a little crazy. But she'd been right all along!

Galen was... was something!

And these puppies... they'd been sleeping by the door every single night, just like always. And every night around three AM, she was awoken to the silence of the room and the shadows cast by their glowing ruby eyes. Except for tonight. Galen had woken her instead.

Her mind raced, and the sweat from her panicked sprint was cooling on her forehead.

What did she do?

She needed to get out of here. Before Galen came back.

Maeve didn't want to see him. Not now. Not before she could... process. But like hell was she hanging around waiting for Galen to fucking sacrifice her or something!

Without giving herself any time to talk herself out of the decision, she pulled open one of the drawers below her and unveiled the doggy treats.

Taking a handful, she lowered her hand low enough to let the pups sniff.

Their excitement tripled, little barks echoing around the kitchen as she teased them.

"Go get 'em!" she said, throwing the treats into the living room.

The pups rushed after them, and she heard the thumps as they raced too fast and skid across the hardwood floor.

They were still acting like dumb little puppies, even if they were demon dogs.

She jumped from the island and sprinted through the kitchen archway, past the couch and to the bedroom. Slamming the door, she twisted the lock before turning to face the room.

Her stomach churned as she looked at the bed, the sheets still mussed from their sleep. And other activities. But the ache between her legs was reminder enough.

She lifted a hand to her lips in realization.

The shadows. It hadn't been a trick of light. The wings were Galen's. And the horns.

"How did I get myself into this?" she asked.

Stop it. Pack now. Questions later.

Maeve listened to her internal voice for once and tore open the closet door, grabbing her duffle from the top shelf.

She scooped as many clothes as she needed into the bag. It only took moments for her to race around the room and collect the few things she would need.

What the actual fuck?

Tears welled as she reduced her entire life to a single bag and zipped it closed.

This was her apartment. Her furniture. Her home.

A home she'd decided to share with Galen. But he wasn't even...

She shook her head. She didn't remember demons being included in mythical creatures that actually exist. Vampires and werewolves, fairies and whatnot. But demons?

The rips... the weird hours and the mysterious boss and the wings. She couldn't explain those away.

"Is he the devil?" she whispered. "My boyfriend is the fucking devil!"

Grabbing her bag, she grit her teeth as she faced the door. All she had to do was get past the dogs, get in her car, and drive.

Where was she going? She had no idea, but away was sounding pretty damn good.

No one would ever believe her if she tried to tell them. And by the time she did get someone to listen, Galen would probably be long gone. Or worse, it would piss him off and he'd have to kill her for telling his secret.

Her best bet would be to leave. Possibly the city.

Galen knew everything about her. Her friends, her family, her favorite places. He would know where to look to find her if he wanted to.

If.

Why would a demon want to date a human? Was it some kind of sacrificial thing?

She wasn't even a virgin!

With a huff and a shake of her head, she grabbed her bag and rested her hand on the doorknob. She knew the puppies were in there, just waiting for her to leave. Their whines were echoing around the apartment, making her heart and head hurt. But in the end, they were just puppies. Even if they were demon dog puppies.

She could simply walk past them and leave.

Maeve sucked in a deep breath, dried her tears, and pulled the door open.

The puppies rushed in right past her where she was hiding behind the door.

Even better.

The three of them tripped over each other as they slowed down, but before they could redirect themselves, Maeve slipped out and slammed the door behind them.

They went to yelping and barking on the other side, and it broke her heart a little to leave them there.

But that was Galen's problem now! He shouldn't have brought home three *demon* dogs in the first place.

With a grunt of frustration, she turned her back on the bedroom and marched across the living room, eager to get in her car and leave this all beh—

The lock on the door rattled only once, not even long enough for her to do anything but freeze, before it opened.

Galen stood on the other side, face and forehead sweaty like it had been that night he'd had a nightmare.

So had he run off to the alley and grown wings then too? Was that it? He'd lied about that as well?

The alarm ringing through her was echoed in Galen's expression as he saw her, his grin wilting and gaze dropping to the bag in her hands.

"Maeve?" His voice was soft, innocent. Confused.

She rocked the bag behind her legs, gripping it with both hands behind her back. She couldn't tell him she knew.

Lie.

"I was going to go stay with, uh... Amanda for a few days."

He lifted those dark eyes to hers, and they were filled with suspicion. She swallowed, stepping back from the door. From him.

"Amanda? Haven't heard that name in a while. Is everything okay?"

Galen wasn't buying it. It was in his tone, his expression.

Maeve came up with the quickest lie of her life. "She's having marital problems. Requested a girls' day."

"For like a week?" he asked, nodding at the full duffle bag. "And at four in the morning?"

He stepped into the apartment and shut the door, leaning back against it.

The ball in her stomach grew spikes.

"A girl's gotta have options, y'know?" she said with a laugh that didn't sound like herself at all.

Galen studied her for the longest moment, his expression hardened like a cement block. He gave nothing away, and Maeve did her best to hide everything.

She huffed. "Besides, not like you can talk, Mr. Long Walks in the Middle of the Night!"

Galen lifted a hand and pinched the bridge of his nose. "Fuck," he said, paired with a bang as he knocked his head back against the door. "How'd you find out?"

The question caught her off guard. Not just the words, but the tone. As if she'd ruined her own surprise party. Not as if she'd found...

Found...

Maeve cocked her head to the side, choosing to play dumb. "What do you mean?"

Galen lowered his head, one brow arched high. "Come on, I'm not stupid. What gave it away? Was it the shirts? I just kept forgetting to take them off before I... Maybe I am stupid." He groaned aloud to himself, and Maeve kept quiet.

She didn't know what to do. She didn't want to admit it. Was it bad for her to know? What if that was a death sentence?

Was she going to die?

No. Galen wouldn't let anything happen to her.

Right?

Unbidden, her throat grew tight with emotion, and she turned her head to the side. She squeezed her fingers around the bag and cursed her luck.

If she'd just packed a little bit faster.

If she'd not followed him in the first place, if she'd been content with her ignorance.

If only she... hadn't swiped right.

"Just... let me go stay with Amanda," she choked out, gaze heavy on the curtains to her right. She couldn't look at him.

But they both knew what she was asking. He could read between the lines.

"I can't do that," he said, voice hard. "I can't."

The finality in his tone made her heart sink, and she swallowed, closed her eyes, refused to face him. It pushed a tear down her cheek, and she angrily brushed the offensive wetness away.

Maeve was not going to cry.

If she was going to die because she had shitty taste in men, the last thing she wanted to do was give him the satisfaction of her tears.

"Maeve... you're mine," he said softly, "and I won't let you go, not without letting me explain."

Her gaze snapped open. "Explain what?" she asked, finally facing him.

His expression was stricken. "Explain what's going on. I'm sure you have a lot of questions," he said reasonably.

Reasonably. As if the devil wasn't standing in her living room. As if she hadn't been dating him for the past year.

As if he didn't go into dark alleys and grow a pair of horns and veiny wings and disappear into a cloud of smoke like something out of a horror movie.

Maeve finally lifted her gaze to him, studying his expression. Unbidden, her gaze drew upward, searching his dark waves for any hint of horn. She'd never felt anything while she'd run her fingers through his hair.

But... She blinked away the image that burned itself into her mind. Where were they?

"I can hide them," Galen whispered, and she dropped her gaze back to his.

He ran a hand through his waves. "Can't very well blend in with them out, can I?" he asked with a wry smile.

Maeve huffed out a breath, still at a loss for words. She didn't know what to say, how to act.

She narrowed her gaze on Galen. The man she'd dated for the last year. They had inside jokes. They did couple things that no one else did. She cooked his favorite meal, and he baked her favorite brownies. They got drunk, and they'd embarrassed each other, and she'd yelled at him and he'd growled at her and—

If she could do all that then why was it so different now? He'd been a demon this whole fucking time?

He could have killed her already!

What the fuck was she so scared of?

Dropping the bag to the ground with a thump, she crossed her arms.

"What the fuck is going on?" she demanded.

10. An Invitation

Galen

His heart, ancient as it was, still ran just fine, Galen would like to report. It hadn't stopped racing since he'd walked in the door, found Maeve with a bag packed big enough to... to leave. Because she *knew*. She'd found out. And she didn't want anything to do with him.

But she didn't know the whole story. She didn't know the truth, she only had her own misconceptions to go off of.

Galen wasn't going to let her leave without learning everything. Not now. Not when finally—

Of course, once she had every fact, if she still...

If she still wanted to leave *after* she had all the facts...

That was Maeve's decision.

The Maeve in front of him, the one demanding to know what the fuck was going on. That was his Maeve. That familiar spark in her eyes, ready to flay him alive if he didn't listen.

He felt his lips twitch, affection swelling in his chest as he stared at her, arms crossed and expression broadcasting much the same.

And suddenly, he didn't know what to say.

"Uh…" His brain sputtered like an old car, but nothing came out.

"Unbelievable," she spat through gritted teeth. "You don't even have anything to say?"

He leapt into action as Maeve leaned down to grab her bag.

"Okay, okay!" he urged, holding out a hand. "I just need a second to… collect my thoughts."

"*You* do?" she shrieked, snapping back up with a finger pointed in his direction. He winced. "My boyfriend just sprouted horns and wings and *you're* the one who needs a minute? Ugh!"

Well, when she put it like that…

Any second now, steam was going to trickle from her ears. He just knew it.

"Fine! I'm a demon!" he shouted, aiming to get the words in before her fucking temper exploded and she ate his soul.

And that was coming from someone who knew someone who actually *did* eat souls.

"Yes, I gathered that much, thank you. And?" She rolled her hand, motioning for him to get on with it.

"I mean… that's it? What do you want? I don't know where to start."

"The beginning works," she suggested dryly.

Okay, so all he had to do was tell her everything she thought about the afterlife was wrong. Great. "Of my life? Uh… are you in the mind-set to have all your beliefs challenged and possibly proven wrong?"

Humans loved their beliefs, and more power to them, but Galen wasn't actively trying to stress Maeve out. Telling her Heaven and Hell actually existed might be a lot.

"Galen, I'm atheist!" she argued. "You know this! I don't have any beliefs."

Pinching the bridge of his nose, Galen took a deep breath. "That's my point. I think we should sit down," he suggested.

"That is literally the last thing I need to do right now," she retorted. "I don't want to be still. You sit down."

Galen did. Maybe he was the one who wasn't handling this well.

As he began to speak, Maeve mapped her trail out in the living room, beginning to pace. Tension lined her shoulders, and beneath all the anger and snappy remarks was *Maeve*. Scared and unsure. He had to remember that.

"I was born an angel. Fun fact."

Her steps faltered by the window, and he paused to wait for a question. It was still dark out, still the middle of the night. Seemed appropriate for all the secrets he was about to spill. But she didn't say anything, didn't even face his direction. All he got was a wave of her hand to continue.

"That didn't work out, obviously. So I fell. That's why my coloring is weird."

"The color of what?"

"Me. Well... demon me. My skin and wings and horns and stuff."

She turned to him slowly. "To be fair, I was kind of blinded by your LED light show, so I didn't really get a chance to study you in the shadows of the sketchy alleyway."

"Oh," was all he could come up with, paired with a wince. "I can show you again?" he offered, slyly glancing up to see her reaction.

Her glare was trained in his direction.

So that's a no.

Galen clasped his hands together and braced his forearms against his knees. But his face was aimed in Maeve's direction, studying her reactions as he talked.

"Does it hurt?" she asked.

He paused. "Changing into a demon?"

She nodded once, and even after Galen was turning her world upside down, she was still concerned for him.

Fuck, he loved her so much.

"It doesn't hurt. Just kind of tingles."

"Okay. Go on, keep talking," she urged, but the panic was gone from her voice.

"After I fell, I landed in Hell, but it's not like... lava and burning people alive all the time. It's nothing like they teach here. And it's not like being an outcast either. Yeah, it is kind of like a demotion, but it's more like... ah, how do I explain it?" He racked his brain for a good analogy. "Like changing locations at a job. It's like I started working at a different office. And when I got to the new office, I started out at the bottom of the totem pole. Until now. I've finally worked my way up to where I want to be." Should he even tell her the good news?

"So the promotion shit was real?" she asked, having trekked her way near the door again, staring at him.

He frowned. "Yeah. I've been working my ass off."

"So you *work* in Hell? What do you do?"

He scratched a hand through his hair, already missing his horns.

"Right now I process all the paperwork for transferring souls. But the promotion... I'll be more like an overseer. A manager. Less hands on and more delegating. More time off. And—"

He cut himself off, getting too excited about the possibilities. But it was Maeve he needed for those possibilities to even matter. Without Maeve, the promotion was nothing. She just didn't know it.

"And what?"

His cheeks heated. "You can't be mean to me when I tell you," he warned.

Maeve spun on him. "For someone who's lied the entire time I've known you, you're expecting a lot."

Galen swallowed. "Yeah, you're right. It's just... going to sound silly. It's not like human customs."

"Tell me!" she urged.

Rolling his eyes, he secretly rejoiced. If she still wanted to hear about something that embarrassed him for possible ammo, that meant she still expected to be around to use that ammo, yeah?

Galen just had to be truthful. This was his only chance.

"Even though Hell isn't all fire and flame, demons still don't have free rein. We only work. There's no, uhm... dating. Or marriage. At all. There's no reason to when you're lower rank, because the population would be out of control otherwise. So... only demons in specific positions have earned, uhm... permission."

"Permission to do what? Find a demon honey?"

"Ugh, no," he grumbled, covering his flaming cheeks. "To date. To find a partner and get married and all that shit. To have a life. We only exist as working bodies, and that's it. That's why the promotion was such a big deal. I finally got to come topside and... and find you."

Dropping his hands, he lifted his gaze to study her. On the other side of the coffee table, near the front door, she stared at him with a carefully blank expression. His chest squeezed. This was worse than her anger.

Then she finally spoke. "So that's the real reason you were on Ring'r, huh? To wife someone up," she teased with a laugh that didn't sound like it was filled with humor. "I wouldn't expect a... a demon to want to settle down." Another dry laugh scraped past her lips.

He couldn't laugh with her, because she was right. He'd used that app specifically once he'd learned about it. Apparently, everyone knew Ring'r was the serious dating app. You went there searching for long-term relationships and commitment instead of hookups and one-night stands.

Her eyes were wide as she stared at him from across the room. The disbelief on her face made his heart ache.

"I got the promotion," he said softly.

The room was silent. No cheering or kisses on the cheek or swooping Maeve up in his arms to celebrate.

"I'm now Devil of the Seventh Region of Hell," he said. If only she understood what a big deal it was.

Her eyes grew wide. "I have no idea what that means." She lifted her hands and raked them through her hair. "I don't think I want to know what that means. Aren't you... I mean, you're the Devil!"

His breath escaped him in a wheezing laugh. "No! No, no. Don't—I cannot stress this enough—do not get me confused with The Devil, capital T. That's not me. In fact, I'm much lower ranking than that. Can't even touch him." Well, now he just sounded like a loser.

"No, stop. Let me restart," he asked, rubbing a hand over his brow. "I'm not The Devil. I'm not Lucifer, the ruler of Hell. Though he doesn't really do much ruling anymore, since we do all the work..."

"Getting off track," Maeve interjected.

Galen nodded, waving a hand through the air. "Anyway, just like at a huge company, there's the CEO—Lucifer. Then there are all the managers and regional managers and HR, and then there are all the employees that do the day-to-day things. You know?" Proud of himself for the accurate analogy, he glanced up eagerly, ready to see the light of understanding in Maeve's gaze.

Instead, he found a blank stare. "And?" she asked.

"And... I'm like a regional manager of the Seventh Region. So I just make sure all the demons who report to me are doing their job right."

"What is their job? What is your job? Don't you like... dip people in lava for eternity or something?" She barked out a laugh as she rounded the recliner. "This is fucking ridiculous. A demon. A devil even. Of course I would match with the only fucking demon on the whole goddamned app!"

She was shouting by the end of it, and she deflated quickly, dropping down in the chair and burying her head in her hands.

"This can't be real."

He wished he could... goddammit. He would rip his heart out for her if Maeve would only request it. "But it is," he urged. "I'm real, and so are we. That's why I wanted to tell you, to make sure there were no secrets between us. Maeve..." He trailed off and slid across the couch, dropped to his knees before her, hovering a hand over her leg before gently placing it down.

She didn't flinch away. That was a good sign, right?

Galen's heart pounded in his chest. "Please, let me explain more. How can I make this easier?"

He was seconds away from fucking begging.

If someone told him ten years ago that he'd be on his knees about to beg a human to give him another chance, he would have laughed in their face. And yet, here he was, lump in his throat and a boulder in his belly.

"Then why did you wait until I found out to explain everything?"

"I wanted to wait until I was certain the promotion was mine. I didn't think you would figure it out. And I... it just so happens that I have the promotion now."

Maeve was quiet for a long time. His thumb stroked a soft rhythm over the shape of her knee as he waited. And waited.

"You're really shitty at hiding stuff," she said, her laugh choked out. "You kept leaving your shirts in the trash after you... changed. Where your wings ripped them. I thought I was going crazy."

Galen's eyes fluttered shut, chest heaving with a painful breath. "No, Maeve. I'm just... a fucking idiot."

"You were chanting. To the puppies. And their eyes glowed." She lifted her head, pinning him with a knowing glance. "They're not normal puppies, are they?"

"No," he admitted. "They are going to guard the gates of Hell when they are old enough."

"Like Cerberus? The three-headed dog from Greek mythology?"

"Yeah!" he said. "How'd you—"

"I searched Google for answers, Galen! Like Google was going to tell me you were a demon. But I *knew* something was up. I even—" She choked her words off, eyes wide, and dropped her head back into her hands.

Was that a blush on her cheeks?

"Maeve, what'd you do?" he asked, biting his cheeks at the smile threatening to curl his lips.

"Nothing," she lied. Her voice was small, and Galen sighed, letting her keep her secrets for now.

"You're not crazy. There *was* something up. Me being a shit demon, for one," he added, aiming for levity.

"Are you evil?" she asked finally, voice softer than he'd ever heard it.

It scared him.

"I don't like to think so," he answered honestly, softly, and hoping with every fiber of his being she believed him. "I was born this way. I'm not a human who went to Hell and became a demon. That's not how it works. I... Can I show you?" She wouldn't look at him, and it was killing him.

"Show me what?"

"Hell. It's not what you've been envisioning your whole life."

"What?" Maeve asked with a shout and drew back from his touch. She finally met his gaze, but there was fear in her eyes. "I don't want to go to Hell!"

"No harm will come to you. I swear," he promised. "Hell's not all that bad."

She dropped her gaze to her lap with a sigh. "There's no going back from this, is there? Now that you've told me your secret, do you have to kill me?"

His chest seized at the thought.

"Absolutely not," he answered, his voice almost a bark. She shrunk back into the recliner, and he lowered his voice. "Nothing will happen to you. I swear it. Not here, and not in Hell. It's not all fires and lakes of lava. It's not what you've been told, not what all the mythologies in the world could touch."

"If it's not dangerous for me to know, then why were demons excluded from the Big Reveal, huh? Vampires, witches, werewolves, sure, fine. But demons were never mentioned."

He sighed, wringing his hands together. "We thought demons might be a little... much, for the human population. What with Hell and all."

"Can't say I blame you there," she muttered, gaze flicking to her feet and back up.

He watched the spark of interest flicker to life behind her eyes.

"So you're... a prince of darkness?" she asked. "You're important there?"

"Not to toot my own horn, but yeah, kinda. Though that is Lucifer's preferred title, so for the love of everything, don't call me that around him."

The blood drained from her cheeks. "I have to m-meet Lucifer?"

He stared at her. "Who else would marry us?"

"M-Marry? Is this a proposal?" Her gaze was wider than ever.

"What? No! Don't ruin the moment! The proposal is going to be so special you won't even know it's coming." Galen was messing this all up. None of this was going how it was supposed to!

"Oh really?" she asked, crossing her arms.

He nodded confidently. Of course it was going to be special. It was a proposal—

"Like my surprise party from last year?"

His confidence plummeted at the mention of the disaster he'd created on her previous birthday. "I said I was sorry, okay? I got too excited."

The soft smile that slowly grew on her cheeks made his heart flutter. He was a goddamned devil, and he'd been brought to his knees by this simply stunning, beautiful human.

But then her smile slipped away, and he wished he could bring it back to life.

She groaned and stood, stepping around him and threading her fingers through her hair. He watched as she paced away from him. "This is so..."

He wanted that smile back, turned to follow her with his gaze, still on his knees. "I'm still Galen, Maeve. I'm still me."

"But you're... How can I joke around with a—a demon?"

Galen drew in a deep breath. "You're thinking of a demon how you've always been taught. Evil enemies of the angels and God and out to destroy the world. But it's not... we're not like that. That's not our purpose."

She turned to him. "What is a demon's purpose then?"

Galen rose to his feet, but let Maeve keep her comfortable distance from him. "Please let me show you. I promise, nothing and no one will harm you. Afterwards, if you still don't..." He trailed off, clearing his throat. "If you still think we're all evil, you won't ever have to see me again."

"Because you're going to kill me?" she asked in a small voice.

With a sigh, Galen lowered his head. "No, you stubborn woman. I'd bring you back here and we'd part ways like normal people do during... when they split up."

"I can come back here even after I go there? I won't be stuck? Do I have to die?"

Galen pinched the bridge of his nose. This was all new to her. He needed patience. "Yes, you can leave whenever you want. No dying required. I can bring you back in the blink of an eye, Maeve."

He waited until she met his gaze before he spoke. "I will not hurt you in any way. I want to protect you."

Her usual spring green gaze was dark with a storm of emotions. Concern clashed with anger, and hurt battled with disbelief.

But Galen had to make her see.

"So?" he prompted, holding his hand out for her. "You gonna go to Hell with me?"

11. To Hell We Go

Maeve

Maeve had always been a little... weird. She could admit it now, as an adult looking back on her experiences. Hell, she worked as tech support for customers at a fucking dildo manufacturer. Couldn't get weirder than that.

But weird was... weird was refusing to match your socks because you liked the randomization. Weird was liking sugar on your cornflakes even though it made them *way* too sweet.

She wasn't ready for *my boyfriend's a devil* weird!

But she didn't say no. She thought about it. Staring at Galen, she read the sincerity in his expression. Maeve had seen it with her own eyes.

"What does it feel like?" she asked.

Galen tilted his head to the side. "What?"

"Going to Hell. Are we getting there the same way you did in the alley? In a puff of smoke?" Maeve couldn't *stop* seeing it. Did it hurt? Getting zapped or whatever to wherever Hell was.

"Oh, yeah, but it doesn't hurt. It just... happens. Though I can't go there looking like this," he said, motioning to himself.

Her throat went dry. "You have to get the wings back out?"

Galen's lips twitched at her wording, but she watched him hide it. "Yeah. Horns too."

Maeve worried her lip. Did she want to go to Hell? Not in so many words. But... she was being seduced by the most desired question in the whole world: what happens after someone dies?

It was something that no one had ever witnessed before. Something no one had ever survived long enough to mark down in history books.

What was waiting for us in the light at the end of the tunnel?

That probably should have been her leading factor for agreeing to go with Galen to Hell. But Maeve hadn't ever really cared about the whole religion thing, never had a reason to.

But now... now she knew she wasn't *crazy.* Knew her boyfriend *had* been hiding something—a big something! Rips in the shirt, the chanting, the weird puppies, his disappearances.

And she wanted more answers. A year wasn't enough time to get to know someone, and that was never more apparent than this moment. But despite everything, she still loved this fucker. Wanted to know every damn thing about him.

Even if it meant—

"So?" Galen prompted. "You gonna go to Hell with me?"

Maeve stared at him from across the room. Galen had been lying throughout their whole relationship. Could she trust him now?

Everything she thought she knew about her partner was wrong. He was a demon!

Who ruined your surprise party last year because he was the worst at reading social cues.

Who'd talked to her when she was upset, and even now, continued putting his socks and dishes in the right places.

She'd never had a boyfriend, a partner, who listened to her like Galen did. Who supported her like Galen did. Who loved her and made her life easier and more fun instead of stressful and difficult. Galen was the best boyfriend she'd ever had, demon be damned.

The man who cuddled those silly puppies couldn't be an evil demon.

The same man who made her coffee and left it on the counter for her, made to perfection, couldn't hurt her.

She could... Maeve truly felt like Galen wouldn't let anything happen to her.

And dammit, the answer to all her questions stood a few feet from her, hand held out, awaiting her answer.

"Let's go to Hell," she murmured an answer.

She reached out to take Galen's hand, her palm slipping into his like it always belonged there.

Maeve discovered something about herself that night.

Apparently, she was into demons.

When he told her to close her eyes, the air grew... tense. Like when you stepped outside right before it stormed, and the wind was blowing and the leaves were rustling and the sky was gray and you knew something was coming. Goosebumps tickled her skin as Galen put his wings on.

But it wasn't *just* wings. She felt his skin vibrate beneath her touch where she held his hand, and the *very* specific sound of fabric ripping. Galen's hand tensed in hers.

"Oops. I forgot about the shirt again," he whispered.

It took everything in her for Maeve not to burst out laughing like a schoolgirl during an exam.

When the vibration stopped only seconds later, Galen squeezed her hand gently. "Whenever you're ready."

Blame it on her messed up sense of humor. Her lack of sleep. Hell, call her plain crazy.

But the first thought that went through her mind when she finally blinked her eyes open and saw Galen was...

Yeah. I'd fuck that.

Maeve didn't know what she had imagined a demon would look like. But it wasn't anything like the one in front of her.

"You're gold." But he wasn't a new, bright, and shiny gold. He was... tarnished. Like an elegant vase worn from lack of any care in a long, long time.

When he smirked, his teeth seemed sharper. "Congratulations, you know your colors."

Maeve dropped his hand and walked around him. His gold wings were similar to what she thought bat wings looked like.

"It really is from the wings. I knew there was something up with all your shirts," she admitted. "Crazy, my ass."

Galen frowned. "How long have you known?"

Maeve's cheeks heated. She didn't want to tell him about the little tests she'd put him through. That wasn't really pertinent information, was it?

"A few weeks. The shirts were weird. And chanting to the puppies? Then there was the dream." She gasped. "That's right! It wasn't a dream, was it? You totally ran off in the rain to do demon stuff."

He winced. Guilty.

"I'm sorry. To be fair, I didn't *want* to hide it from you. But I couldn't tell you either. I got so sloppy, I'm sorry. I should have been more careful." Guilt carved out a furrow in his brow, and her first instinct was to comfort.

"You were stressed about the promotion," she said automatically, and then shushed herself.

No comforting the lying boyfriend. The lying *demon* boyfriend.

Suddenly, she imagined all the times they'd... they'd *destressed* together.

"Oh my god, we've had unprotected sex. You came in me!" she shrieked and cupped her mouth in disbelief. "What if I had gotten pregnant? Would I have had a little demon baby?"

Galen palmed his head, wings twitching in irritation. "We went and got you the shot, babe!"

She sputtered. "Yeah, for humans! What if you have super demon sperm or something? How can you be sure? Has that ever happened before?"

"No," Galen answered with a sigh. His wings moved with him, like they were their own entity. Was he controlling each muscle in them? "A demon has never gotten a human pregnant. Not by accident."

"So it *can* happen?" she asked, narrowing her gaze, undeterred by her curiosity.

Galen groaned. "Yes, it *can*, but only under very special, controlled circumstances. Babies aren't accidents in Hell."

"Oh."

He was so sure. And she couldn't really argue with facts. And besides... Maeve glanced at his wings.

Tarnished gold like the rest of him. "Can I touch them?" she asked.

They twitched as if in answer. "Uh... sure. Just be careful."

"Why? They don't look fragile or anyth—"

As she touched the webbing of the wing, it jerked and furled closer to Galen's body, snapping away from her touch. "They're ticklish," Galen explained, clearing his throat.

That made her want to touch them more. "That seems like an unnecessary weakness," she mused.

Galen nodded. "Yeah, it's what you could call our consequence of leaving Heaven. I used to have white feathers to protect them, but when I fell... so did they."

"So this was beneath the feathers all along?" she asked.

"Yep. Ever wondered what an angel looked like? Just imagine me, but shinier and with fluffy wings. You're welcome. Instead of twelve eyeballs, I have twelve inches of—"

Maeve slapped her hand over his mouth. "Don't say it," she warned, trying to hide her smile.

Gaze trailing upward, Maeve studied his horns. They were the same tarnished gold, but were mostly obscured by his dark curls. "Can I see those closer?"

Without warning, Galen wrapped his arms around her waist and hoisted her up high. Instinctively, she wrapped her legs around him and looped her arms around his neck for balance. "That's one way to do it," she commented breathlessly.

Galen had always lifted her with minimal effort, but something about him doing it right *then* made her breath catch.

Is it because you know he's a demon now? Dangerous?

Maeve accidentally let a snort slip out and covered her mouth. Galen was a demon. But he wasn't dangerous. His fucking wings were ticklish!

"What's so funny?" Galen asked, voice muffled.

Pulling back, Maeve put a few inches between his face and her chest so he'd at least hear her.

"Just thinking about the possibility of you being dangerous." His smile slipped, and she continued, "And I decided it wasn't very likely."

"I'm not sure if I should take that as a compliment or an insult."

"Well, I haven't run away screaming yet, have I?"

"There's still time," Galen mused, tightening his arms around her.

Maeve smacked him lightly against the shoulder and ruffled a few of his curls. "Come on, I wanna see these horns of yours."

"Alright, alright." Galen lifted her a little higher until she could see the top of his head.

The horns extended from both temples and curled around the sides of his head, ending in a curved point. They were gold at the base and darkened along his head to blend in with his hair.

Maeve ruffled his curls again, frowning as her fingers bumped into the hard horns.

"Well, now how am I supposed to pull your hair with these in the way?" she wondered idly, grabbing them both in her hands like... well, like horns.

Galen moaned.

Maeve paused.

Oh.

Oh.

Maeve tapped Galen on the shoulder, and when he lowered her down, she learned that yes, demons could blush too.

"We'll be exploring that later," Maeve promised.

Her gaze landed on something flickering behind Galen's back, and her eyes widened.

"Is that... a *tail*?" she whispered.

Galen stiffened, the color on his cheeks deepening. "Maybe."

"Where's that been hiding? Is it ticklish too?"

He huffed in the most adorable way... you know, for a demon. "In my pants? And no, it's just kind of... there."

Maeve's lips twitched into a grin as it swirled behind him. "Do you control it?"

In answer, it curled around him, and Maeve followed it with her gaze as it drifted closer, before it tapped her on the shoulder. It was long, with a little spade at the tip, and gold just like the rest of him.

"You're like a cat," she announced.

Rolling his eyes, Galen didn't exactly argue, cheeks still showing pink even through his golden skin. "So, that means you aren't super weirded out and mad?"

"Oh, I am very weirded out," she corrected, stepping away. "And yeah, maybe a smidge pissed that you've been lying this whole time." His face fell, and she felt like she'd just kicked a puppy. "But I get why you had to do it. Doesn't mean I like it. But I get it."

Galen nodded, though the crestfallen look melted away. "So are you ready for more?"

"You mean it's actually time to go to Hell now that you've changed outfits?"

"Oh my god," Galen groaned, tilting his head to the ceiling for patience.

Did he ask God or Lucifer for it?

"Gotta make sure you look nice for Daddy Lucifer?"

"Maeve, I swear," he said, shaking his head.

"What? Say it. Don't be a pus—"

Galen wrapped his arm around her waist mid-sentence, and the rest of her words were swallowed by... by whatever he did to make them leave the comfort of her apartment and...

"Are we flying?" Maeve screeched, wrapping her arms around his neck. Over his shoulder, she watched his wings flap, could feel the muscles in his body move to accommodate their weight.

"I'd say so," Galen shouted into the wind. Asshole. She held on tighter as he *flew* them to their destination.

Which was Hell.

And apparently only accessible through a supernatural tunnel for *flying demons.*

The wind was hard against her back, so she kept her head tucked into Galen's chest until his wings changed pace. She just *felt* it in the way his body moved, the way they slowed down, like when an elevator neared the correct floor.

Her skin tingled as they came to a stop, and she lifted her head. Galen was lowering them, but it was only once they landed that Maeve was able to see what was ahead of them.

An archway stretched high above them, clearly meant for giants. Glancing back over her shoulder, all she saw was darkness. In there somewhere was their apartment.

"What was that?"

Galen chuckled. "The highway to Hell."

"I can't stand you," Maeve lied as she gripped his hand tight and faced forward.

With his hand wrapped around hers, Galen stepped forward. "Welcome to Hell."

12. Getting Off Easy

Maeve

Little sparks danced all over her skin as she walked beneath the archway, and she shivered them away.

Galen pulled them to a stop once they were inside, wide smile curled as he waved a hand out. "Well?"

Maeve's eyes widened as she took in the endless hallway stretched out in front of her, gray walls and pristine white floors and low, ethereal lighting. And doorways. More doorways than she could count. Granted, they were *huge* doorways and halls to accommodate their rather—she watched as a demon disappeared through one of the openings, wings and all—*large* inhabitants.

"Try not to talk to anyone. I'm gonna show you around, but it's important we stay out of the way of operations."

"And what exactly *are* operations?" Maeve asked, curious. So far, no fires or lava. Just golden flying demons.

"I'm gonna show you. Stay close, okay? It's really easy to get lost, and even harder to be found."

Maeve gulped. Her sense of direction had always been lacking anyway.

She twined her fingers tightly with Galen's and glued herself to his side. From the corner of her eye, she watched him smile down at her.

And who was he to make her melt like that, huh?

A wing sidled up on her right, effectively giving her a Galen-shaped shield.

She wanted to cry.

Their steps moved in sync as Maeve let Galen start their journey. They went straight down the hallway, and they only passed a few doors before Maeve was peeking around Galen's wing to see what was inside.

It was so... weird. It was just people sitting there staring blankly into space.

They passed a pair of demons, whose conversation trailed off as they approached. Maeve was struck silly. They looked different than Galen. Their horns were a different shape, and one was short and stocky while the other was thin and waiflike.

"Galen," the small one said, nodding his head in hello. The other followed suit. Their gazes flicked to her, their hands, and then away before they beelined to their destination. She frowned.

Oblivious to her musings, Galen continued. "It's like I told you. Hell isn't what you think it is, but the point *is* to suffer. I mean, dipping people in lava is fun and all, but then there's the screaming and the ones that panic could get *really* loud and it's just... there's an easier way to do everything, yeah?"

Maeve stared up at him. "Did *you* dip people in lava?"

Galen glanced at her out of the corner of his eye. "Uh... From your tone I'm gonna go with... no?"

Her mouth dropped open, and Galen winced. "Listen, it was my job, okay? But we're all past that now, and look how peaceful it is. You hear that?" he asked, lifting his hands to gesture to the endless, plain hallway.

"Uh... no, I don't hear anything," she said. Nothing but the sound of her racing heart.

"That's my point," Galen said with a smile. "It's quiet."

Maeve didn't know what to say.

"The lava stuff was centuries ago. We don't do that anymore. Now, each person gets their own personal hell... inside their head. That's the best way I can explain it. So the only lakes of fire and lava now are brought on by their own horrors."

Tugging him to a stop, Maeve pointed to the next room that they passed. Inside, a middle-aged woman sat on the same metal chair that was in every room. "Centuries, huh? We'll be revisiting that. What's she doing?"

Galen stepped forward, his wing bumping Maeve to come with him. She jumped at the soft contact and followed him into the eerily silent room.

All he had to do was look at the woman before he answered, "She's stuck in a crowded supermarket with a list of items that are across the store from each other."

That's it? "Okay... but why is she here?"

He winced. "You sure you wanna know?"

Without giving herself time to rethink it, she nodded.

"Well, she didn't care for the animals she was in charge of, resulting in her own death, and many of those inside the kennels."

She gasped. "That's awful."

"And to her? So is the supermarket."

Those poor animals. And their owners? "The supermarket doesn't seem bad enough."

He glanced to her with a proud gleam in his eye. Should a demon's praise give her butterflies?

Probably not, but their wings fluttered in her belly just the same.

"To her it is. Want to see?"

Maeve met his gaze, unsure of her answer. But it *was* just a supermarket.

"Is it safe?" she asked.

Galen rolled his eyes at her. "I wouldn't let you get hurt."

"Fine, fine. Yes." Dammit. Curiosity killed the cat. Hopefully it wouldn't kill her.

He placed a fingertip against the woman's forehead and held the other hand out to her. Carefully, she placed her palm in his care.

She gasped as the gray walls and the white floor swirled into nothing, the dull lights and the boring floors and the never-ending corridor all disappeared. What took its place was... just as Galen had said. A supermarket.

She was shoved to the side by a bickering mother, whose face was just a blur. No identity. No mouth, yet her voice carried just the same. In fact...

Turning her head, she found more of the same. Blank faces, yet their voices carried, lifted to the fluorescent lit ceiling, and bounced around in a deafening roar. Like a Walmart on Black Friday, but worse. A list appeared in her hand, and it was in that moment Maeve realized she was experiencing what the other woman was.

The list contained things like diapers, then ketchup. Then hair bows, bread. It went back and forth, items listed in the most chaotic order, making the woman rush across the store just to have to rush back through the pushing crowd and the buggies taking up too much room and the voices kept getting louder but she couldn't talk to any of them and—what isle was she supposed to be on? What item was she supposed to be looking for next?

And why wouldn't this line just move?

Maeve gasped as the vision disappeared and the original room took shape around her once again. Dropping her hand from Galen's, she placed it against her chest and felt her racing heart.

"She has to do that for eternity. Every time the list is completed, it just adds new items for her to have to collect."

"That's no ordinary supermarket," she remarked.

He nodded. "Yeah. It's Hell. Every punishment is curated for each person. They each get to live in their own hell for eternity. There's no day and night. No sun and moon. No... essence of the time passing."

Her heart thumped in her chest.

"So they just sit in those rooms? Stuck in their heads forever?"

"Yep."

That did sound hellish.

But she guessed that was the whole point, wasn't it?

"How come you're allowed to leave? Why aren't you stuck here?"

Galen squeezed her hand. "Earth is an extension of Hell, simply referring to any place God doesn't reside. That's why we're allowed to exist there, because he's in Heaven. But obviously when it comes to going back and forth, there are rules because we don't want our secrets getting out."

"Did you break a rule by telling me?" she wondered aloud. The last thing she wanted was him getting in trouble.

But he shook his head before her worries could ever manifest.

"Why not? Seems pretty serious, telling a human about something like this."

"Because I love you," he said confidently and met her gaze.

It took her breath away.

"That's the perk of becoming the Seventh Devil of the Seventh Region of Hell. I'm allowed to look for a partner. So I did. And I found you."

"But aren't you just now getting promoted?" They'd been fretting over this promotion for months. "We've been dating for over a year!"

"Well, yes. But, we'll just keep that to ourselves, hmm?" he suggested, adding a wink. "Besides, I'm not the only one bending the rules a bit. We used to have dragons."

"Dragons?" Maeve squeaked. A flash of an image, great big wings and a spew of fire. She blinked.

"Yeah, but they are long gone. It's been close to a century. But that—I'm getting sidetracked, none of that matters now though, as I am finally allowed to wed." He looked proud at this announcement.

"Yes, you mentioned that," Maeve responded dryly.

Galen ignored her, grabbing her hand again and ushering her along with his wing. If it wasn't so cute, she probably would have been annoyed.

"So does everyone know you're the big boss now?" she asked as another demon passed, nodding respectfully at Galen. None of them seemed alarmed that a human was walking amongst them.

"Yeah, it's been announced. That's actually why... why I had to leave last night," he admitted, squeezing his fingers around hers. "Lucifer requested my presence, and I couldn't say no. I just didn't know it was because he was going to shake my hand and congratulate me."

Maeve arched a brow. "Is it a big deal to see Lucifer?"

"Of course! He's my boss. He just rules from... afar. Very afar. It's rare that we actually see him. And if he requests your presence for anything other than a promotion or a marriage... good luck." Galen winced, and Maeve wondered just how scary Lucifer had to be to make *Galen* nervous. He seemed pretty damned invincible with his golden skin and fancy horns and huge wings.

She didn't like the idea of *any*one hurting Galen, devil be damned.

Galen led her around Hell, down hallway after hallway, room after room. She met a few demons and expended enough blood from blushing that it was a miracle she didn't pass out. They were all so fucking *polite*. All 'yes ma'am,' and 'you take care of him' and the newest one...

"Wow, surprised Galen could talk to women after all," a deep voice teased.

She arched a brow at the brave words, gaze flitting between the two demons.

"You made for good practice, Julian," Galen responded dryly.

Which was just hilarious. Apparently, as the two of them broke out into chuckles before hugging. Galen's wing left her side for a split second, and she felt utterly exposed.

"This is Maeve," Galen announced as he stepped back. His wing curled right back around her, and Maeve inched closer to Galen's side while trying to look like the super tough cool human girlfriend she was.

"Lovely to meet you, Maeve. I've heard a lot about you," Julian greeted, tipping his head at her with a smile. He was handsome, with hair cut close to his head and just as tall as Galen. His horns were curved straight up. No hiding those.

Maeve racked her brain. Something about the name Julian rang a bell, but she couldn't quite pin why—

It hit her.

"Julian! The one who recommended you for the promotion?"

"That's me," Julian claimed with a proud smile. "Glad to see he's taking advantage of the benefits."

"Har, har," Galen interjected. "I'm pretty sure Julian has somewhere to *be*, doesn't he?"

Julian's chuckle was silky smooth. "For once, you're actually right. I have a summons to deliver."

Galen blinked at that. "From—"

"Yep. The king himself," he answered wryly.

"Why?"

Summons weren't good, right? That was what Galen had said. So if it wasn't a wedding or a promotion...

"Dunno. Just following orders." The demon suddenly turned his attention to Maeve. "It was lovely to meet you, Maeve. See ya!"

"Bye... Julian," she answered, frowning at the sudden tension in Galen.

Galen urged her along and patted Julian on the shoulder before whisking her away.

"Should we talk about that?" she suggested, but Julian's chuckle echoed down the hall, and Galen distracted her with a painting.

Yeah. In Hell. Hanging in the hall like a decoration.

The *only* decoration. Maeve was getting kind of tired of Hell. It was all the same. How did they not get bored here? Were they just accustomed to it?

"This is the new wing," Galen explained, and took her down another hall, leaving the quickly crowding corridor. All of the rooms in the new area were bare, without chairs or dead people living in nightmares.

Galen, excitedly talking about the recent expansion of the section they were touring, walked right past a room filled with several demons. Maeve was busy taking everything in, even them, so it didn't fall on deaf ears when one of them sneered, "Goody-two-shoes Galen finally got his promotion. How long before he pops the question on some unsuspecting human?" That got him a round of chuckles from his buddies, and as Galen stopped to tell her about some fancy painting and whose blood it was painted in, she listened more to the group.

"Oh, he's got to go for a nun. He needs someone else who's got a stick up their ass."

Her mouth dropped open. *Galen* had a stick up his ass?

Galen, who glanced over at her, and seeing her mouth hanging open, laughed. "I know! It's pretty amazing, isn't it?" he asked, staring up at the painting. Then he continued outlining plans for the area.

Okay. So maybe she could see it.

"No, you've got it all wrong," a third voice chimed in. "He needs someone who's going to take the stick *out* of his ass."

Her brow furrowed as irritation sparked into anger. Galen was a dork, sure. But he was her dork. And wasn't he everyone's boss now? What assholes!

"Why are we still talking about this?" One of them groaned. "Who cares? Besides, I'd watch your mouth because rumor is, he's visiting today."

"Fucking hate that. Again?" someone complained.

Her cheeks turned red with irritation.

Galen babbled on about Hell, so without thinking, she leaned her head around the corner, their attention locking on her in an instant. "Yeah, he is, and this unsuspecting human doesn't appreciate how you're speaking about your fucking superior," she spat.

Four pairs of eyes narrowed on her, the flap of their wings shuffling against their backs staining the silence.

"If you have a problem, you should bring it up with management, fuckface," she added, cheeks burning with anger. And a little embarrassment, because in her moment of anger she may or may not have forgotten that these were *demons*, and she might have bitten off more than she could chew.

The closest one took a step toward her, but she bravely stood her ground. Not even a demon was going to intimidate her. Maeve parted her lips for one more retort, to really twist the knife deep, but his lips parted, and a growl tumbled out, and—

Something obscured her view, wrapping around her and pulling her back into a hard chest.

"That's enough," Galen barked, his voice vibrating against her back.

Maeve waited until Galen was finished chewing the group out, and even *her* cheeks were burning with shame once he got done. Jesus. No wonder the guy was the seventh whatever of the... whatevers. Maybe she should have paid closer attention.

Footsteps filled the room as the group shuffled silently past them, properly chastised.

When the last of them were gone, Maeve scraped a finger over the wing wrapped around her.

"Hey!" Galen warned, unfurling his wing and flapping it out before it closed up accordion style to hang at his back.

"I can't believe you just took me under your wing like that. Literally."

He rolled his eyes. "Well, someone had to shut you up before that asshole overreacted."

She crossed her arms. "He deserved it."

"Oh, of that I have no doubt," Galen agreed. A moment later, he let out a sigh. "Listen, I know your immense rage could fuel a small country in the human realm—"

"I take that as a compliment," she interjected.

"—but these are *demons,* not rednecks in the movie theater parking lot. *And* I'm in charge of you. Doesn't look too good on my first day as Seventh Devil of the Seventh Region of Hell if my girlfriend goes around beating up lowly demons, does it?"

Maeve crossed her arms. "Couldn't very well let them talk shit about the Seventh Devil of the Seventh Region of Hell, could I?"

"Don't you make fun of me," he warned, but met her gaze with a sparkle in those dark depths.

His soft gaze always made her melt in a puddle.

Maeve understood the sincerity of the situation. She'd messed up.

"I'm sorry for letting my temper get the best of me. Again…" Maeve cleared her throat. "I didn't mean to embarrass you in front of your… uh, peers. Coworkers. Underlings?"

Galen's lips were twitching as he stared down at her, and she averted her gaze. "So, like, if you need to ritualistically fuck me in front of them on an altar or something to really put me in my place, I totally understand." She nodded. Yeah, what a noble offering.

"Oh, is that what you'd want?" he asked, tugging her tightly against him and wrapping his wings around them. Most of the light from the room was blocked out, and Maeve could barely see him in the dim light. They were in their own world.

She bit her lip. "What I *want* is for you to apologize for lying."

Even though I lied too, like, trying to poison him and stuff. Oops.

His face fell, and she couldn't keep up the ruse any longer. "By making me come no less than… seven times."

Gaze darkening, Galen curled his lips in a slow smile. "Seven?"

"Yep," Maeve said, popping the 'P'. "Because you're the Seventh Devil of the Sev—"

"—nth Region of Hell," they finished together.

"You're getting off easy if you ask me," Maeve teased.

Galen rolled his eyes. "You're getting off even easier."

13. The Tour

Maeve

But that didn't stop him from unfurling his wings and leading her down the hallway through another maze she lost track of in the first three minutes.

"Where are we going?" she asked. They were passing less and less demons. Were they going deeper into Hell?

"My office. Wanna see it?"

Maeve expected something fancy with windows. But where would the window look out into? So it made sense, even if it was slightly disappointing, that the office was the same gray walls and white floors, though the desk and many papers scattered across it added something different to the room.

"My favorite aspect, personally, is this," Galen said, grabbing the door handle of the first door she'd seen since they'd arrived and closing it. Unfortunately, the light went with it. Only a thin sliver glowed beneath the door, and Maeve heard a click of metal.

"Oh, a lock too?" she asked, bringing a hand to her chest. "You spoil me."

Galen's hands framed her waist, backed her toward the desk, and Maeve slipped up onto its surface when her thighs hit the back of it. He towered over her as he came closer, unfurrowing his wings.

She felt like a giggling schoolgirl, stomach aflutter and pulse racing as his dark silhouette, barely visible in the soft glow, covered her. He dragged his lips against hers, leaving her breathless as she arched up into him and roamed her hands over his pecs, his shoulders.

In the barely there light of the room, Maeve let Galen strip her naked. When she urged him to follow, she heard the sound of fabric ripping, and she tutted.

"Come on, the shirt was a goner anyway."

"You need to stop ripping them all. Before you know it, you won't have anything left. Then you'd have to walk around shirtless all the time." Maeve sought him out, fingers brushing against the abs she knew like a map. "That would be such a shame," she remarked, sliding her hands up his chest.

"You'd be looking at me like a piece of meat, like you are now."

Maeve gaped. "What? How would you know? It's too dark in here!"

Galen chuckled as he slid to his knees. "You just told me."

Before Maeve could snap back, Galen pulled her to the edge of the desk and cupped her ass like a bowl. With no hesitation, he dragged his tongue along her folds, making her jerk against his hold, buck against his face as he tasted her like a starving man.

She threaded her hands through his hair, careful to avoid the horns and feeling the familiar soft strands between her fingers. Maeve was saving that for later.

With the practice of a man who knew her inside and out, Galen tongued her clit and dug his nails into her ass, encouraging and marking. Maeve let him hear her moans and shaky breaths, letting him know how good he was being, how fucking perfect he was.

Galen tilted her into him, tightened his grip on her ass, hummed into her in the most delicious way and—

Her first orgasm bled into the horizon as she snapped her eyes closed and rocked her hips against Galen's face. He trailed a hand up her stomach to her breast, her achy, sensitive nipple. His hand was so warm against her skin it burned, and when he plucked at her nipple, piercing and all, she cried out. Her pussy clenched as the added sensation tipped her further to—

The edge drifted away as Galen stopped, pressing a kiss against her inner thigh, hand trailing away from her breast.

"What the fuck was that?" she asked once she'd caught her breath and gotten over the shock. "Did you just edge me?"

She felt his triumphant smile curl against her skin.

"I think the agreement was to get you off seven times. You didn't say when."

"You're such a brat," Maeve grumbled, realizing the corner she'd locked herself into, and let her head drop to the desk with a thunk. But like, what was she going to do? Tell him *not* to give her seven orgasms? Unacceptable.

Rolling her hips up into him, she tried to urge him for more. She'd been so close, it wouldn't take much—

"I'm sorry," Galen teased. "But I fail to see how this is a bad thing. You get seven orgasms. What do I get?"

"To watch me *have* seven orgasms. Duh," she snapped.

"Well, that's not the answer I wanted to hear," he rumbled from down by her hip bone, words skipping across her skin like stones across a pond.

They sank like boulders against the harsh waters of her impatience. "Well, that's the only one you're getting for now."

"Feisty," he murmured. She jumped as he nudged his nose against the crease of her thigh.

"Always," she answered. "Do you not have *any* light in here?"

"Since my office is still kind of new, I don't have a light... unless you want to open the door."

Her breath caught, and he noticed, fingers spanning the back of each thigh.

"Hmm. Maybe you weren't kidding about the whole sacrificial altar sex. Do you have an exhibition kink we haven't explored yet?"

"No," she claimed, yet her pulse raced faster at just the idea.

Galen was gone in a whisper of air, and Maeve was gravely still against the desk as she heard him rustling around.

"Right here," he warned, voice close to her, before he tugged her off the desk and rearranged her in his lap. With her back to his bare chest, Maeve was spread out over him, balanced so that when he spread his knees, her legs parted wider. He was dressed from the waist down, while she remained totally bare.

Something warm, rope-like wrapped around her ankle—*his tail*—and tugged her leg a little wider.

The cool air lapped between her legs, and she felt how wet she was in comparison.

Smoothing his hands over her exposed skin, Galen traced and learned her shape in the dark until she was lax against him. Every time he skated close to her nipples, dragging his nails across the weight of her breasts, she wanted to beg to be touched. She needed him to touch her, but every time, he just took it away from her.

"There's no sacrificial sex altar, I'm sorry to disappoint. But if you're really dedicated, we could just pull the door open."

Her fingers twitched where she had them dug into the sides of Galen's thighs.

"So we don't hate that idea? Hmm."

Galen sighed, his chest expanding behind her. "But you saw how few demons there are down here. We'd be lucky if anyone passed by. Even if they did..." He trailed his fingers down her sides, where she was *almost* ticklish, sending goosebumps melting across her skin.

If they did, they'd have to find her sprawled out over Galen's lap like this as she arched into him and waited for his touch, *any* touch.

"They'd hear you first, probably," Galen continued, spreading his touch out over her knees and dragging his fingers back up the insides of her thighs. "Depending on how loud you are."

"Well, that depends on if you're actually going to do anyth—" The word dissolved into a high-pitched breath as Galen dragged the backs of his knuckles over the sensitive flesh between her thighs.

The rough fabric of his pants irritated her skin, but that just made it feel better to move. And she tried, but he only parted his knees more, his tail pulling her legs wider and taking away any power she had.

Galen always suffered so nicely for her. And in those moments, Maeve swore that the next time Galen was in charge she was going to be just as perfect for him.

Well, here was her fucking chance. So she took a deep breath, stilled herself, and waited for Galen like she was supposed to. And finally, *finally*, Galen brushed the pad of a finger between her wet folds. He hummed, the sound rumbling at her back, an affirmation of sorts, and it fed her need.

He stroked all the way to her core only to spread her arousal around, dragging the sensation back up to her clit. Maeve jerked as he centered all of his attention on that bundle of nerves, teasing her with the crest of pleasure, waiting just until it was within sight, just when her breath was hitching and her eyes were drifting closed, to stop.

Again.

And again.

Until Maeve lost count and was covered in a sheen of sweat and dripping down his fingers and writhing on his lap.

There was something so intimate about trusting someone else with her wants and needs, her pleasure. And something even more intimate in finally letting go, finally submitting to the ease of it all. She could let go with Galen, be as needy or demanding as she wanted, and he was always so good for her in return. Letting Galen see her come apart—*really* come apart—was what he deserved. Hell, it was the reward he earned for making her feel so fucking good. And dammit, Maeve needed it too, and Galen was the one she trusted to give it to her.

"Please," Maeve whined. "Hasn't it been long enough?"

"For what?" he asked.

A shiver danced up her spine as the cold air skated across her skin, and she was still quivering from the almost there and—

"Galen, let me come," she pleaded, lifting her hands up to loop them around his neck. She brushed her fingers through the short hairs at the back of his neck.

"You do sound pretty sweet when you beg so nicely," he murmured, voice rocky.

"I can be so much sweeter if you just... *Oh...*" She trailed off as his hand drifted across her thigh, practically holding her breath.

"I'll be the judge of that," he promised before laying his hand between her thighs and stroking her clit.

She looped her own fingers to keep from clawing up Galen's neck and parted her lips, letting out every moan and whine that he drew from her mouth.

It took seconds, if that, for him to center on where she needed him and stroke his middle finger in a repetitive motion. It was constant and perfect, and lightning was gathering across her skin and her lips parted on a cry, silenced by Galen's hand over her mouth as she came.

It struck, stilling her for a half second as she split apart on the inside, cunt quivering as Galen worked her through it.

Galen removed his hand from her mouth, framing her jaw and tilting her up to him. His lips crashed down on hers as he drank the pleasure straight from her mouth.

He only gave her a breath to recover before he sought to pull another from her.

A finger pressed at her core before he pushed inside. She clenched around him as he surged deeper, pressing down on her stomach with the palm of his other hand while crooking his digit within her. Maeve hadn't even caught her breath from the first before the second hit. It sizzled across her senses, made her bear down on Galen and shake in his arms.

A sheen of sweat began to chill on her skin, and Galen lifted her up, guiding her to straddle his knee so they were face to face. The threaded material of his jeans was coarse against her sensitive flesh, but the pressure was the loveliest friction.

"Ride me," he demanded.

Or not.

Maeve wasn't in the headspace to question him, so she palmed his shoulders, and he steadied her around the waist.

And Maeve chased her own goddamn orgasm on Galen's thigh, rocking back and forth until the overstimulation became exactly what she needed. Just as her well-earned orgasm was cresting over the horizon, Galen lifted her away from his thigh, from the friction she needed.

"Wait—fuck you," she growled, grabbing at his shoulders and clawing because using words to say she *needed* was too difficult.

"I know," Galen purred sweetly. But she didn't want sweet.

She was desperate and she needed—

"Yes!" she shouted as Galen finally got it right and slid first one, and with her desperate moan, two fingers inside her. She rocked her hips on him, rutted against his hand because he'd said, "Ride me," in that irresistible voice, and her thighs were already shaky, and she silently begged him not to pull away again.

But he didn't, and she gave herself the third orgasm in the palm of Galen's hand, letting her head fall to his shoulder as she panted.

"Galen," she whined, her own voice wrecked and unrecognizable. "You have to fuck me," she stated it as a fact, but it came out like a plea. "I want you inside me," she begged, tightening her grip on his shoulders. "I don't want it if you're not inside me next."

"Green or red request?" he asked, leaning his head against hers.

Green, meaning it was a request he was still allowed to ignore for the sake of the scene. Red request meant it was nonnegotiable, and Maeve would fucking *die* if he didn't do whatever she asked of him right fucking then.

"Red," she said, because she was spoiled, and she didn't want him to touch her clit anymore. At least not for like ten seconds.

Galen—clearly the one with better eyesight here—pulled her up and placed a hand against her lower back to bend her over the lip of the desk. The most comfortable way to settle was with her knees on either side of Galen's thighs, balanced precariously over his lap and the small gap between the desk and chair.

It put her on absolute display for him, and she shivered as he palmed her ass with both hands and kneaded her cheeks.

Maeve didn't even know when he'd lifted her up to undo his pants and drag them halfway down his thighs, but all she knew was that he palmed her hips and pulled her back toward him. The blunt head of his cock poised at her core for a split second before he dragged her down onto him, plunging deep inside.

The fourth orgasm was the most powerful, as she finally had something to squeeze around and grind on as she whined. It tore through her with a force that left her legs weak after, but she knew they still weren't done.

As soon as she stopped quivering around him, Galen lifted her up before guiding her back onto him with a hand on the small of her back.

Bracing her forearms on the desk, Maeve muffled her cries in her skin as Galen dragged her on and off him. With his size, any angle was a good angle, but every time she was pulled back onto his length, she felt the punch of him with every breath.

It was too much. It was way too much, the way her pulse thrummed through every part of her body and rushed in her ears. But it was too fucking good to stop, and they were already more than halfway there, and every time she moved, her breasts dragged against the desk, the metal of her piercings clicking against the wood and adding even more kerosene to the fire she couldn't control even if she wanted to.

Burning up from the inside out, Maeve bounced on Galen's cock with his help, though he wasn't allowing her to go any slower or faster than he wanted.

"You feel so good," Maeve breathed, trying to tilt her hips for more leverage.

Galen knocked his elbow against her knee, making her lose her balance and sink farther down on his cock. "Don't rush," he warned.

"Okay, okay, okay," she promised, slowing back down to the pace he wanted.

It made her simmer. Like she was stuck in limbo and unable to drag herself closer to orgasm but unable to stop because it felt too good, and she swore if she just had... *something*, she could come again and—

It hit her out of nowhere, as Galen's hands suddenly tightened on her hips and held her in place while he bucked up into her, fucking her through the warm wave of the fifth with sharp, delightfully harsh movements. Their skin smacked together, filling the room with such urgency, such volume, she feared someone *would* come knocking to see what the hell they were doing.

His tail curled around her thigh, the spade dragging up her skin closer and closer. He dipped it between her thighs, brushed with the lightest pressure over her clit, and dragged the sixth from her with a surprised shout and a jolt. Her eyes fluttered closed as he strummed her clit along with his movements, shaking in his lap. Then he spun her around until she was staring down at him, barely lit from the light beneath the doorway.

She tilted her head back as he entered her again. Maeve began rocking on him, chasing the last one because she knew he was going to give it to her.

"You have to come too," Maeve demanded raggedly, nails digging into his shoulders. Her breath punched from her throat with each thrust. "Please, please, please, I wanna feel you inside me." The words forced themselves between her teeth as she battled with oversensitivity.

It occurred to her that she could fake it. Whose idea was it to go for seven? Maeve didn't even know if she *could* have another one.

But she listened to Galen's mumbled words in the background. How she was being so good for him and how much he loved this, each sweet praise paired with a kick of his hips.

And somehow, Maeve reached that final orgasm with a cry of relief as its gentle warmth filled her from head to toe. Body tensing, cunt pulsing around his cock, Maeve *still* had the sense to reach up and wrap her hands around Galen's horns, holding them as she rocked her hips against him.

His groan was muffled in her neck as his pace faltered. She clung to Galen with what little sense she had left as he followed after her, filled her, warm and soothing, like a balm to the fire she couldn't resist playing with. Her eyes drifted closed as her body officially melted, slumping against Galen's chest.

"That's right, baby," Galen cooed, kissing his way across her chest and throat.

She untangled her fingers from Galen's horns, limp with bliss. They breathed together for a long moment, Galen peppering little kisses all over her face, until she pushed him away with a giggle. Blinking up at him, she tried to clear the fog of pleasure.

Until the only thing left was one glaring realization that jolted into her with the ooze of horror.

"Galen," she whispered. "I left the puppies locked in our room."

So that was how Maeve got carried out of Hell tucked against Galen's chest, hidden by his wings so she could go rescue her favorite pillow from the sharp teeth of demon puppies.

And no. Not a single soul was brave enough to ask the Seventh Devil of the Seventh Region of Hell why he was shirtless.

14. Confession

Maeve

"Wait, wait. So this list," he said, swallowing a laugh and trying to compose himself. "How long was it?"

Maeve felt her cheeks heat and spooned up another bite of ice cream. Her hair was still wet from the bath Galen had run for them once they'd returned home and confirmed the puppies' proof of life.

They'd been napping on the bed. No sign of chaos, other than a few new scratches on the door and a sacrificed shoe.

One of Galen's, she'd been relieved to discover.

Currently, the puppies were beneath her feet against the bar, staring up at her and awaiting any melted drops she might spill.

Now that she knew everything... Now that Galen was standing in the kitchen with his own bowl of Moose Tracks, wings tucked away, she felt even more embarrassed for listening to some silly list from the internet.

"Out with it," he demanded, tapping his spoon against the bowl. "What did the internet tell you to do?"

"Ugh!" she groaned, dropping her head and stabbing her ice cream. "It was so stupid. But I was onto something the whole time! And I stand by that." When she earned nothing but an expression that screamed, 'Really?' she huffed. "The website listed five things that were supposed to out you. Or like, repel you."

She winced when Galen broke his composure with another laugh. "Oh, I'm loving this," he declared between bouts of laughter. Maeve's lips tightened into a thin line, and once he saw the expression on her face, he stood up straight and cleared his throat. "So... what was on the list?"

"Like hell I'm telling you. You're just gonna laugh at me," she whined.

Galen closed the space between them and sat his bowl down before leaning toward her with his palms flat on the counter.

"I'm not gonna laugh," he promised. "I'm just extremely curious. I mean, hello, if you figured it out, so will other people. I need to warn the other demons that have moved up here."

Narrowing her eyes, Maeve studied him. He seemed sincere.

"What happens if a demon gets found out?" she asked.

"If we catch it early enough, they have to return and stay in Hell until it's safe."

"That doesn't sound so bad," she mused.

Galen snorted derisively. "Yeah, but it is. They have to stay down there until everyone they were connected to in the human world passes. No connections."

Maeve blinked. "Do you have to kill the humans?"

"What? No! Maeve!" he scolded, cheeks red.

What was she supposed to think? Maeve held her palms up in a shrug. "What? You told me you used to dip people in lava!"

"Used to! We're past that now. Past it," he urged, waving his hand aggressively. "But it's sad, and it's a lot of unnecessary mourning."

With a sigh, she spooned up another peanut butter cup and narrowed her gaze at him. "Fine. But no laughing."

"Scout's honor," he said, holding up three fingers.

He was definitely gonna laugh.

Maeve rolled her eyes before steeling herself. "The first thing it listed was salt. Said some mumbo jumbo about purity and shit. But a salt circle seemed a little too obvious. And it never specifically told me how I should use the salt—"

"Honey bun, did you try to poison me?" he asked calmly, a smile twitching on his lips.

"It was just once!" she retorted. "I just oversalted your plate a little."

Galen parted his lips once before snapping his mouth shut and tightening his lips into a line. At first she thought he was angry, disappointed—and how dare that actually offend her?—but as he snorted back a laugh, she felt her cheeks grow hot.

"Are you laughing at me?" she yelled, majorly offended. "You said you wouldn't!"

"I'm sorry, I just—I suffered through that whole meal so I didn't hurt your feelings," he confessed. "You said it was a new recipe, and I felt bad. How mean." He pouted.

"Oh shut up, it's not like it killed you," she drawled. Maeve couldn't let him see how sweet she thought he was. Dammit.

"A little salt? No, it just turned my bloodstream into the Dead Sea," he drawled.

"Oh, don't be dramatic," she sassed. "Do you wanna know the second trial or not?"

"Do I ever," he told her, and pulled out the other bar chair to sit beside her. He hooked his bare foot around the bottom rung on her chair and tugged her closer.

"Part two was silver, though I didn't end up getting around to it until the end," she admitted when he nudged her with his elbow.

His mouth made an audible pop as it dropped open, and his gaze lowered to her cleavage.

"Yeah, it's what you think," she admitted with a groan, staring up at the ceiling. "I bought silver body jewelry. Figured if you were a werewolf you couldn't suck on my titties with the silver in."

She watched the mirth begin to glow in his gaze, and she narrowed her eyes in challenge. "Well, it worked, didn't it? You're welcome. I rocked your world with that new titty jewelry. Confirmed it, not a werewolf."

Maeve tried not to remember all the details of how exactly *he'd* rocked her world that night. She definitely wasn't recalling how she tugged on the thin chain attached to each nipple, making her quiver while he was inside her.

"The third one was iron," she announced, distracting herself from those thoughts. There was no way she was having another orgasm.

Galen didn't seem to have the same reservations, and he spread his legs a little more on the chair, staring up at her in a challenge.

Do not jump his bones, she told herself.

No bones jumping.

Nuh-uh.

"Iron. Cast iron. Same thing, right? But you didn't flinch when you got the cornbread off the counter for me. Haha, funny," she said, waving her spirit fingers.

"I think your mythology is a little... off," he pointed out. She shot him a glare.

"So... I assume the fourth had something to do with cleaning out your grandmother's chest?"

Rolling her eyes at her transparency, she nodded. "Yeah. Religious relics didn't work either."

He chuckled. "They normally don't. What was the last one?"

Maeve paused, remembering the last and final option and eating her last bite of ice cream to console herself. She was about to sound extra psycho. "Five wasn't an option, even from the beginning, I'd like to note. And after the jewelry, I let it go. I accepted that maybe I was the crazy one and you were definitely normal and there was no reason I needed to even go through with the first four trials. So that was when I decided to forget it altogether."

"When we did the scene," he said, putting the pieces together.

She hummed in affirmation. "I was relieved even though I was frustrated." A dreamy smile curled her lips at the memory as she pulled the spoon from between her lips to get every last sugary drop. "And it's always fun to put you in your place," she said, glancing at him from beneath her lashes.

Galen's eyes met hers and darkened. Then he was off his bar stool and sliding his hands around her waist and squeezing. "Maeve," he murmured reverently. He lowered his head to her neck, and she paused, found herself tilting her head up to give him more room.

Having a demon boyfriend was pretty cool so far.

"What was the fifth trial?" he asked, and then pulled back with a grin.

That fucking tease.

"No, I'm not telling you because it was stupid anyway. Reading it almost turned me off the article altogether, but believe it or not, my resources were slim."

"Then it should be no big deal to tell me what it was," he pressed.

"Why do you wanna know so badly?" she challenged.

Galen's smile widened. "I want all the ammo I can get so I can hold this over you for the rest of our lives."

"But I was right! So technically it's on you that you weren't better about hiding it," she pointed out. Her heart was pounding though. The rest of *our* lives? Galen wanted that?

"Come on, Maeve, please tell me?" he asked, dragging out her name dramatically. "I have to know all the details. This is too good."

"Oh, so this is just a big amusing story to you? Glad to know I was panicking and freaking out and you're having a big laugh about it all."

He pulled her to the edge of the chair and tilted her head back. Way back, until she was staring straight up at him. "Baby, you know that's not what I meant."

Maeve didn't know what it was about Galen. Even now, knowing what he was... she wanted him. Not just because his touch left the heat of sparks behind and his new—to her—horns were erogenous zones. It was because he was so sincere and dorky and could make her laugh for hours. She relaxed in his hold, absorbed his warmth with a funny kind of relief.

"I know," she admitted. "I'm just being difficult because I'm embarrassed." She rolled her eyes, trying to distract from the way her cheeks were heating up.

"Don't be embarrassed, love," he murmured. "It was really brave. I mean, what were you gonna do if I ended up failing one of the trials, like silver? You would have thought I was a werewolf. And then what? It's pretty badass."

Maeve bit down on her smile, pretended to think it over with a hum. "I don't know. I guess I would have resorted to the fifth option, a machete," she deadpanned.

Galen froze, his entire body tensing for a long moment before he loosened his hold on her and dropped his hands to the chair on either side of her hips. Then he began shaking, and she startled at first before she realized he was... laughing.

She continued on. "I suppose the writers were thinking if I couldn't figure out what you were, a beheading was appropriate no matter what," she mused.

He finally let her go, his composure disintegrating as laughter burst out of him in a loud boom. It was a rare kind of laugh that she didn't get to hear every day.

Unable to resist, her lips curled up into a wide grin, watching as Galen put a hand on his stomach. "It hurts," he hissed between chuckles. "A machete? Really?"

"I swear," she promised. "I could pull up the site if you wanna see—"

Galen cut her off with a wave of his hand. "No, no, please don't. I can only take so much," he said, finally catching his breath. "It's gold. I love this," he admitted, gaze landing on her. He wiped a tear away.

"I love you," he said a moment later, words slower, laced with intention.

Her breath caught. She'd heard those same words from Galen before many, many times. Maeve didn't know what it was about this time that was different.

Maybe because... there were finally no more secrets between them.

Maeve was the one who pulled him closer this time. "I love you too. Next time, don't make me google how to discover your secrets. Just tell me, yeah?" she suggested.

"I know that *now*. I just didn't think it would go this well. I've been freaking out for weeks, wondering what you were going to say."

"This definitely wasn't what I expected when I swiped right on you," she teased. "I didn't think I'd have to learn how to date a demon."

Galen hummed as if in thought. "Did you forget the part where you tried to poison and maim me? I'd say you learned how *not* to date a demon, if anything."

Maeve gasped dramatically. "Galen!"

"But that's okay," he continued. "I'll give you a second chance."

"Unbelievable," Maeve murmured, a smile etching itself onto her lips. Maeve tugged Galen down to her.

Before their lips could meet, sharp little teeth nipped her big toe, and she squeaked, yanking herself back to see which little damn pup it was this time—

"Eli!" she grumbled. "No toes!"

Maeve lifted her glare to Galen, who melted it right off her face with a kiss born of overwhelming affection. When he pulled away a long moment later, Maeve smiled up at him dreamily.

"Ready for bed?" he offered.

"Oh my fucking—" She moaned, wrapping her arms around his neck. "I'll finally get a whole night of sleep. Eight interrupted hours. Now we're talking."

Galen chuckled and pulled her limp form off the chair like she weighed no more than a doll. "Anything to make you moan like that again," he teased.

"Take me to my chambers, *oh* Seventh Regio—no, it's Region Seven—*no*, Demon Seven of the—"

"—don't hurt yourself, honey."

"Shut up," Maeve grumbled.

"Make me," Galen retorted.

Maeve tightened her arms around his neck and waited until he was lowering her to the bed before she made her move. Reaching up, she stroked one of the horns he'd left on display since they'd gotten home, pulling a moan from him.

His cheeks flamed red.

Maeve kissed the blush tinting his skin. "Be careful what you wish for."

Maeve

"Alright, that's it," Maeve announced, slamming her laptop closed.

Galen paused on his way to the kitchen, arching a brow at her shaped in curiosity. "What's it?"

She stood, tossing her laptop to the side and stalking to her boyfriend. His sly grin was a little too calculated, and she knew then she'd played right into his hands.

Stupid gray sweatpants.

Stupid hot demon boyfriend.

He backed into the doorframe and stayed there as she approached, until she was craning her neck back to stare up at him.

His pretty dark eyes were alight with mischief, and the gold horns on his head glimmered in the soft back light from the kitchen. Rarely did Galen take on his human form anymore, Maeve made sure of it.

"Get on your knees," she demanded.

He arched a brow at her, but his eyes darkened in interest. "Make me."

Maeve practically purred, reaching up to caress a line down his shadow speckled jaw.

"I don't have to make you do anything, do I, Daddy?"

Galen melted down to his knees without another word.

It was new, the *Daddy* thing. But the first time Maeve had tossed the word around as a tease, Galen turned to putty in her hands, and goddammit, she loved the Seventh Devil of the Seventh Region of Hell more than anything else.

So Daddy it was, sneaking its way into their playtime more often than not.

"You've been walking around in those sweatpants all day. Pretty slutty of you," she observed.

He paused with his lips scant centimeters from her hip, and the bow of them twitched. "Slutty, huh?"

"Don't act like you don't know," she scoffed, and threaded her hand through his dark locks, careful to avoid the horns. "You knew we'd end up here."

With heat building in her core, she dragged him the remaining distance, and his lips brushed against her skin in reverence.

He gazed up at her, eyes dark with arousal and bottom lip sticking to her skin. Another kick of heat landed in her stomach, and she swallowed. "You know what to do, Daddy."

Galen's hum was *so* bratty. She wanted to feel it between her thighs. "Don't know. Memory's kinda fuzzy."

His wings fluttered slowly, curling around them, tips dragging against the floor like a set of claws. Just the sound made shivers dance along her skin, or maybe it was the way Galen nipped the exposed flesh of her hip. Or maybe the way his tail wrapped around her ankle and caressed the skin there.

"I'd be happy to remind you," she answered, staring down at him.

He nodded against her, lips dragging along her skin, and that heat bloomed anew.

"Take my leggings off," she breathed, and in an instant, Galen's claw-tipped fingers were tugging at her waistband, and she was stepping out of the pool of black fabric a heartbeat later.

"Surely you know what to do *now*," she drawled.

"It's coming back to me," he answered dryly.

His hands gripped the backs of each of her thighs as he pulled her legs apart, and she widened her stance.

"If you wanted to get down on your knees so badly," she rasped out, "all you had to do was ask."

"But this is so much more fun," he whispered, the heat of the moment taking their voices away.

She tightened her grip in his hair, decided at the last second to torture him a little, and grabbed onto one of his horns.

Galen's moan filled the apartment, and she was suddenly thankful the puppies were in Hell, where they belonged. Not dead, mind you, just doing their duty of guarding the entrance like Cerberus had once upon a time, and getting spoiled by every demon that walked past.

Most importantly, they were no longer in her apartment, which meant Galen could get on his knees for her any time of the day without being interrupted by three yipping little beasts.

Led by his horns, Galen nosed at the slit of her cunt, tongue darting out to taste her.

"Will you take your shirt off?" he asked on a breath.

Maeve lifted her eyelids and stared down at him. When she didn't answer, he tried again.

"Please."

"Do it yourself," she said.

Galen rolled his eyes—she'd get him back for that—but rose to his feet gracefully like the demon king he was, and brought the hem of her shirt with him. She lifted her arms and the fabric slipped easily over her head.

Her nipples pebbled in the cool air, and she chased the chills away with a shiver. Galen's eyes widened appreciatively, almost humorously, at the way her jewel-adorned breasts swayed with the movement.

After he tossed her shirt toward the couch, he hovered his hands over her chest, lifting his gaze to hers in question.

"You can touch me," she told him.

He chased the shivers away as he cupped her breasts, nipples brushing against his palm and sending sparks of pleasure straight to her core.

This ma—*demon* was so weak for her, and Maeve never ceased to be amazed at the power he allowed her to wield over him.

As he lowered his head, she tilted hers up, and their lips met in the middle. His tongue darted out to swipe along her lower lip.

Heat swirled in her stomach, turning to bright pleasure as he rolled her nipples between his fingers. But she still held all the control, only allowing their tongues to twine once he'd nipped at her lower lip the way she liked.

Their tongues slid together, tangling and teasing.

Galen dragged his touch down her sides, framing her waist with his tarnished gold hands.

She tilted her head back, and he followed along, trailing kisses along her jaw and down her neck, nipping and biting and sucking at the skin until he left marks behind.

Despite her control, Galen was too good to her, and she let a gasp escape, a pleased hum, as he dipped lower and sucked her nipple between his lips.

He darted his tongue out to flick at the jewelry, hands digging into the flesh of her ass and pulling her closer to him, as if he couldn't get enough.

Arousal was bright and shiny in her mind, and she smoothed her hands over his shoulders, frowning at the fabric still covering them. "Off."

A clawed hand left her ass, and she giggled at the sound of the fabric ripping, blinking down at him as he tugged the remnants of the tee away.

"You and your ripped shirts," she sighed.

"There are more important things at the moment than one of the many shirts I own," he retorted, lips brushing against her breast.

"Like getting on your knees?" she urged.

Galen dropped to the floor, knees landing silently. He stared up at her, and Maeve bit her lip, indecisive, but ultimately combed her fingers through his hair and dragged him back to her cunt.

He stared up at her with his dark eyes, and Maeve felt herself get a little lost in them—in him. But then he lowered his head, and she grabbed onto his horns and swallowed a whine as he tasted her again.

"That's it, Daddy," she whispered.

Galen very literally shivered on his knees before her, wings tremoring in response.

He hiked one of her legs over his shoulder, claws digging into plump flesh, and she tossed her head back against the doorjamb—when had they spun around?

He swiped his tongue over her clit before returning with a fervor that took her breath away. Pleasure shimmied down her spine, swirling in her stomach as he sucked the bud between his lips and brushed his tongue over it again and again.

"Yes, yes," she breathed. "You're doing so good. You're gonna make me come, Daddy."

He groaned into her, the sound vibrating against her, and she squirmed in his arms, but he held her still.

"You can touch yourself," she told him.

But instead of dropping one of his hands, he just held on tighter, claws digging in and pinpricking a slight pain that made the pleasure swirl even more beautifully.

She followed it by rocking her hips forward, and his nose bumped her mound as he slid lower.

"Daddy!" she whined, cunt tremoring as her orgasm spun closer, fogging her mind and making her weak in his arms, so she held onto his horns tighter.

He groaned into her, and she wanted more of that sound, more of the way he swiped his tongue against her, tasting her arousal straight from the source and nudging his nose along her clit.

Galen's rhythm left no room for breathing, but Maeve sucked a breath in anyway, and it was at that moment—poised on the silence of an inhale, breath filling her lungs—that the ecstasy swooped in and took her away.

Her exhale turned into a moan as she shook in Galen's arms, as she gripped his horns tighter. He groaned into her wetness, and it sent a fresh wave of aftershocks through her before her orgasm had even subsided.

She was panting as she blinked her eyes open, chest heaving, and she realized her knuckles were white from how hard they were wrapped around Galen's horns. Uncurling her fingers, she brushed his hair away from his face and tilted him up to her.

His dark eyes were half-lidded as he let her leg slide off his shoulder, slumping into her with a satisfied sigh.

She chuckled. "Did you come too, Daddy?"

He shivered against her, and frankly, Maeve could do this all day.

His cheek rubbed against her hip as he nodded, and Maeve bit her lip.

She was dating the *hottest* demon king, and she'd fight anyone who tried to say otherwise.

AFTERWORD

Meowdy!!

THANK YOU SO MUCH for reading, and going on this silly, adorable journey with me.

Maeve and Galen have a special place in my heart, and I love them *dearly*.

If you're as obsessed with them as I am and interested in seeing more of them, there's a *ton* of art (spicy and non-spicy) on my Patreon, as well as behind-the-scenes content and early access to new projects and works in progress!

Including book two in Cautionary Tails, which is on its way and available for preorder *now*.

Visit my website to learn more about me, the books I write, Patreon shenanigans, and sign up for The Kitty Letter so you don't miss a thing.

Love, Lana

ACKNOWLEDGMENTS

Kat, my ride or die, for always being there when I needed an ear, whether its for brainstorming or word vomiting about my current hyper fixation.

Thanks Wren for pointing out the craggly bits and helping me brainstorm how to smooth them over.

Sophie, for being just as excited for Maeve & Galen as I am, and bringing them to gorgeous life with your art!

And thank you Meg, for being armed with squees to keep me motivated, and loving this story as much as I do!

ALSO BY

Visit my website to learn more about my books and how to get your
paws on signed paperbacks.
www.lanakoleauthor.com

Cautionary Tails Series
How Not to Date a Demon
How Not to Date a Dragon
How Not to Date a Griffin
How Not to Date an Angel
Crystal Clear Series
Illusion of Escape
Illusion of Death
Illusion of Darkness

The Unlocked Series

Chaos Unlocked

Betrayal Exposed

Misery Undone

Truth Revealed

Hope Lost

Death Defied

Standalones

Feline Good

The Abdominal Snowman

Seasonal Spice & Everything Nice

In the Sweetverse:

Baby + the Late Night Howlers

Lola & the Millionaires part one

Lola & the Millionaires part two

Lyric & the Heartbeats

Fighting Instincts

Bad Alpha

All Packed Up

Faith + the Dead End Devils

Knot That Serious

LANA KOLE WRITING AS LOGAN GREY

Heartbelt Records Series

The Deeper You Go

The Longer You'll Stay

Love in Progress

ABOUT THE AUTHOR

With a southern twang that's all charm, Lana hails from Tennessee with her four feline roommates. If one of them isn't demanding her attention, she's most likely writing. Her stories bring life to characters who don't fit the mold, romance as sweet as it is sexy, and worlds better than this one.

Author of paranormal, sweet omegaverse, monster romance, and queer love stories with a happily ever after.

www.ingramcontent.com/pod-product-compliance
Lightning Source LLC
LaVergne TN
LVHW091258210125
801727LV00020B/172